*"I will send them a ruthless curse
that will make them beg for mercy.
She will be made from Sugar and
spice but nothing nice.
A dram of crocodile tears.
A peck of bird brain.
The tip of an adder's tongue.
Half a pack of lies.
The slyness of a cat.
The vanity of a peacock.
The chatter of a magpie.
The guile of a vixen and the
disposition of a shrew.
And of course the harshest stone
for her heart."*

Gargamel

Punk Rock Nursing Home

Copyright © 2013 by Marcus Blakeston.
All rights reserved.

http://marcusblakeston.wordpress.com
marcus.blakeston@gmail.com

This is a work of fiction. Names, characters, businesses, places, events, and incidents are the product of the author's imagination. Any resemblance to actual persons, living or dead, events, or places is entirely coincidental.

ISBN-13: 978-1491042526

ISBN-10: 1491042524

Also available:

Punk Faction
Skinhead Away
Bare Knuckle Bitch
Meadowside
Biker Sluts versus Flying Saucers

Introduction by Andy T

This story takes place thirty years in the future.

In 1976, in the leafy suburbs of London, a few misguided teenagers decide they want to shock the public with their wacky dress sense. Bin-liners and safety pins are one thing but the use of swastika armbands, for many, is a step too far.

It's only thirty years ago that the Nazi jackboots stamped on the faces of Jewish children. People have very long memories, especially when the scars left by the bombing raids in British towns and cities are still starkly visible.

Thirty years is the mere blink of an eye.

Three years later, in 1979, Margaret Thatcher is elected as Prime Minister. The 1970s have been a long hard slog under a labour government, and many people truly believe any change would be for the better.

The next few years see the systematic destruction of the heart and soul of the British manufacturing industry. Iron, steel and coal production is chopped down to the bare minimum, paving the way for the future mass importation of supplies from foreign countries and mass unemployment here.

The unions are crippled, leaving the hard fought for rights of workers open to abuse from corrupt bosses. Nationalised industries are sold off to the highest bidder, leading to artificial price wars which leave consumers paying higher and higher prices, every year, for essential services such as gas, water and electricity.

With the country on its knees and baying for her blood, Thatcher needs a boost to her popularity to win the next election. Her solution, which works very well, is to sacrifice the lives of thousands of British and Argentinean soldiers in a pointless war.

In 2013 this heartless murdering despot gets a state funeral, paid for by the public purse to the tune of £3.6million. While the Tory government celebrate, millions protest and whilst being ordinary citizens, are labelled anarchists and troublemakers. Her sickening legacy will never be forgotten, and she and her cohorts should never be forgiven.

Thirty odd years is the mere blink of an eye.

Andy T, June 2013

Punk Rock Nursing Home

Colin Baxter strained to hear a Rezillos song above the incessant chatter of the other residents sitting around the communal lounge. Why everyone had to shout at each other when their armchairs were only a foot apart was beyond him. And if everyone was so deaf, or their tinnitus was so loud they couldn't hear themselves converse at a normal volume, why did the music piped into the retirement home's speakers need to be so quiet? It was barely audible.

Colin sighed. He looked down at his entoPAD screen and prodded the Silver Punkers Community Forum icon. He waited for a video advert to finish playing, then scrolled through the subject headings with his gnarled index finger. Most of the posts were adverts for garishly coloured mobility aids. Leopard-skin patterned walking sticks with skull and crossbones handles, pink and yellow mobility scooters with the words Boredom or Nowhere printed on the front basket. Colin wished there was some way to filter out all the nonsense to make the genuine content easier to find.

Frank Sterner shuffled by with his walking frame, making his third trip around the outskirts of the retirement home lounge that morning. Colin watched his slow, ponderous movement past a set of French doors leading out to the back yard. Frank paused in the doorway and looked out before continuing his journey.

Near the lounge door, Fiona Scott sat asleep in her armchair with her mouth hanging open. A line of saliva dripped from her chin. Sitting next to Fiona, Sharon Baker smiled at her entoPAD. She laughed, and held the screen out to Louise Brown on her left. Louise looked, smiled and nodded to Sharon, then turned her attention back to her own entoPAD. Louise wore a pair of headphones, and her white-haired head bobbed from side to side. Her lips formed a string of obscenities as she sang along to whatever it was she was listening to.

Colin wished he had thought to bring his own headphones into the lounge, then he could listen to his own choice of music at whatever volume he liked. But he had left them behind in the dormitory when he got up that morning, and couldn't be bothered going to fetch them. Besides, his bad knee was giving him gyp and he didn't want to put any unnecessary weight on it if he could avoid it.

Colin looked at Greg Lomax, sitting on his right. Greg stared into space, the left side of his face drooped and immobile. The old man hummed tunelessly to himself, only pausing to take a wheezing breath.

"Oi Greg," Colin said, "have you got your headphones on you?"

Greg stopped humming and looked at Colin. "Nrr, Err lrrft thr in thr brrdrrm," he said.

Colin leaned forward so he could catch the attention of Tony Harris, who sat in the next armchair along from Greg Lomax.

"Oi, Tony, have you got your headphones on you?"

Tony shook his head. "No, mate, sorry." His voice sounded muffled beneath the oxygen mask strapped over his mouth and nose.

"No worries," Colin said. He turned to his left, where Dave Turner sat peering at his entoPAD screen through thick jam-jar-bottom spectacles. Dave's hearing aid whistled like the feedback of an electric guitar, in harmony with Greg's humming. Colin decided not to bother asking Dave if he could borrow his hearing aid. Once Colin finished looking through the new posts on Silver Punkers he would just hold the entoPAD against his ear and listen that way.

"Fucking smart," Dave said to himself.

"What's that, mate?" Colin asked.

Dave held his entoPAD out in one shaking hand. Colin glanced at it and smiled. A young child on the entoPAD screen swayed on the bottom rung of a climbing frame surrounded by soft foam mattresses. The child's face was obscured by a full-face safety helmet with chin-guard, and Colin couldn't tell from the thick padded clothes it was wearing whether it was a boy or a girl. Nearby, a young woman in her mid-twenties hovered with her hands outstretched to catch the child should it fall from the climbing frame.

"That's me great-grandson," Dave said. He grinned at Colin through gapped, yellow teeth. "He's three, and he's a right fucking terror."

Colin nodded and smiled back. "Yeah, he looks it."

Dave prodded the young woman on the screen and the video zoomed in on her anxious face. "That's me grandson's missus. Not done too bad for himself, has he?"

"Yeah, I guess."

"Shame they're always so fucking busy, I wouldn't mind meeting them one day."

Colin combed his fingers through strands of white hair on the left side of his otherwise bald, liver-spotted head. He nodded and looked back at the screen of his own entoPAD.

"Yeah. That's the way it goes though, innit? Mine are no different. I used to look after my granny, you know? Back in the day, that is. She's long gone now. Different times, back then. Good time to be young though."

"Fuck, yeah," Dave said. "The best. I wouldn't want to swap it for what the youngsters have got now."

Colin smiled. "Yeah. Their music's shite for one thing.

And there's no dole, so you can't even enjoy yourself like we did."

Dave nodded. "Yeah, good times. You remember that fucking security guard in Woolworths? The one with the limp, reckoned he was in the SAS or somesuch?"

"Yeah, Sergeant Hoppalong. Me and my mate Bri had loads of fun with that cunt. He had a thing about Action Man, used to go fucking ballistic if you messed about with them."

"Yeah?" Dave said. "Wish I'd known that. We used to put on fake Irish accents when we knew he was hovering around. That wound him up no end too."

The lounge door banged open. Colin looked up. A balding, middle-aged man in a white coat pushed a trolley into the room.

"Looks like another new one," Colin said to Dave. "I bet you a biscuit he's on the fucking workfare."

Dave smiled and shook his head. "You must think I'm fucking daft. Of course he will be." He looked down at his entoPAD and went back to watching family videos.

A Lurkers song started playing through the lounge speakers. Colin nodded his head in time with it while he watched the new orderly push the trolley toward Fiona Scott and stand before her. The bald, white-coated man coughed. When Fiona didn't stir from her sleep he shook her by the shoulders and she startled awake.

"Medication time," he said. "What's your name, granny?"

Fiona looked up, but said nothing.

"That's Fiona Scott," Colin called out. "She doesn't really say much."

The man looked at Colin and grunted. He rifled through paper medicine bags on the trolley and picked one out. He tore it open, took out two blue capsules, and dropped them into a small plastic cup. He held the cup out to Fiona for her to take it from him. Fiona's mouth dropped open like a baby bird waiting to be fed. He tipped the capsules into her mouth, pushed them to the back of her throat with his fingers, closed her mouth, then forced her head back until she swallowed them.

Colin shook his head and looked down at his entoPAD. He swiped his finger up the screen to scroll through message headings on the Silver Punkers Community Forum. Hidden among the adverts was a post with the heading Thatcher Day 30 that caught his interest, so he prodded it. Despite only being posted an hour ago, it already had over two hundred replies.

Thatcher Day celebrations, 8th April 2043. Post your memories of that fucking evil bitch here. Never forget, never forgive.

Colin checked the day's date on his entoPAD clock. He smiled when he saw how close it was to the best day of the year.

"Thatcher Day again soon, Dave," Colin said.

Dave looked at Colin. His eyes widened. "What, already? Fuck me, that's come around again quick, hasn't it? It only seems like a few months since the last one."

"Yeah, time's spinning by these days. It's the thirtieth anniversary this year. We should do something special to mark the occasion."

"Like what?"

Colin shrugged. "Dunno. I thought maybe you might have some ideas?"

Dave scratched his head and frowned. A cloud of dandruff settled on his shoulders. "None at all, mate. We could give Thatcher a good kicking?"

Colin shook his head. "Nah, we do that every year. We'll do that as well, of course, but I was thinking something really special. Something we haven't done before."

"What about setting fire to her? Like we did that first year, when the news first broke. Remember that?"

Colin smiled. "Yeah, Ding Dong the Witch is Dead. We had a fucking great party that night at our council estate. Even the little kiddies joined in, it were fucking magic. Maggie Maggie Maggie..."

"Dead, dead, dead!" Dave replied, smiling.

"We're not going to burn Thatcher though. What would we do next year without her? She's the star of the party, for fuck's sake."

"Yeah, good point. I never thought of that."

The middle-aged orderly pushed the medication trolley across the lounge and stood before Greg Lomax. "What's your name, granddad?"

Greg looked up and spoke slowly, with deliberation. Only the right side of his mouth moved, the left drooped down in a frown. "Ir Grrr Limmurr."

The orderly frowned. "You what?" He raised his voice, as if addressing a naughty child. "I said what's your name, granddad. What's. Your. Name? Do. You. Under. Stand. Me?"

"Grrr Limmurr," Greg said, raising his voice to the same volume.

The man sighed and shook his head. He turned to Colin and jerked a thumb at Greg. "What's this one's name then?"

"Greg Lomax," Colin said.

He nodded, then flicked through the medication bags and pulled one out. He tore it open and tipped two white pills and two blue capsules into the palm of his hand. He pushed Greg's head back, prised his mouth open, and dropped all four onto Greg's tongue. Greg spat them out into his right hand as soon as he was released.

"Err cnn drr ir mrrr srll, yrr crnt," Greg said. "Brr ir nrr srrm wrrter."

The bald man looked at Colin.

Colin smiled. "He says he can do it himself, but he needs some water."

"Right, okay." The orderly picked up a water jug from the trolley and filled a small red plastic beaker. "Here. You. Go. Some. Water. For. You."

"Frrr urrrf yrr crnt, err nrr strrpird," Greg said. He pulled a hard plastic straw from his pyjama shirt pocket and popped it in the side of his mouth. He took the beaker and raised it to the straw, sucked up a mouthful of water and glared up at the orderly. He swallowed the four pills, one at a time, while the man stared down at him.

The man grunted, then took the beaker from Greg. He put it down on the trolley and turned to Colin.

"So which one are you then?"

"Colin Baxter."

He found Colin's medication and handed him two blue capsules in a small plastic cup. Colin took them and rolled them around the cup's base.

"You going to take those or do you need help with them?" the man asked, folding his arms.

"I'll need some water," Colin said, "me throat's dry." The orderly grunted and passed him the beaker of water Greg Lomax had used. "You're new, yeah?" Colin asked.

"Yeah, started today."

"Workfare placement?"

He shrugged. "Yeah, so? What's it to you?"

Colin glanced at Dave and smiled. He turned back to

the bald man. "Just wondering."

"Yeah well, just take your medication and don't give me any shit, granddad."

Colin held the man's stare while he tipped the two blue capsules into his mouth. He didn't know what they were for, the only regular medication he had ever needed before moving into the retirement home was for hayfever.

The orderly glared while Colin took a sip of water to wash the capsules down. He nodded, then took the beaker from Colin and put it down on the trolley. He turned to Dave Turner and asked his name.

Colin raised a fist to his mouth and faked a cough as he spat the blue capsules out. He glanced at the bald man, saw he wasn't watching, and transferred the capsules to his dressing gown pocket for later disposal. He looked up and saw Louise Brown watching him from across the room. She smiled and winked. Colin smiled back and nodded.

* * *

Later that night, Colin looked up from his entoPAD when he heard hobnail boots clumping down the hallway toward the dormitory he shared with the other male residents. The retirement home's manager, the only permanent member of staff, on his regular night time prowl before retiring for the evening.

Colin glanced at the clock in the corner of his entoPAD screen, surprised how late it was. The manager was usually tucked up in bed by this time, or doing whatever it was he did up there alone in his upstairs accommodation.

Colin shuffled himself down the bed and lay on his side as the footsteps stamped their way closer to the dormitory door. He slipped his entoPAD under the bedcovers and closed his eyes just before the door creaked open on rusted hinges and the manager shone a torch into the room. The torch's beam flicked from bed to bed, pausing on each resident in turn. When the light fell over Colin he pretended to moan in his sleep and rolled over away from it. He opened his eyes when the torch beam flicked across to Dave Turner's bed.

"Fuck off, you cunt," Dave mumbled. He pulled the bedcovers over his head.

"Get to sleep, Turner," the manager said. "You too Baxter, I know you're still awake."

The manager made another sweep of the dormitory with his torch and turned away. The door creaked shut and his boots echoed away down the hallway. Another door creaked open.

"Louise Brown, what do you think you're doing? Get into bed this instant!"

"Fuck off," came Louise's defiant reply.

Colin smiled and struggled upright in bed. He put his entoPAD face up on a table by the side of the bed and switched on his bedside lamp. He swung his legs out of bed and directed his feet into a pair of Sex Pistols slippers. He reached for his walking stick and pushed himself upright with a grunt. The muscles in his legs ached in protest, and he winced when he felt his bad knee pop. He hobbled over to Dave Turner's bed and sat down on its edge. He reached over and pulled the covers down from Dave's face.

"Dave, you awake?" he whispered. He nudged Dave's shoulder when there was no reply. "Fucking wake up, you old bastard."

Dave snorted and rolled over to face Colin. His eyes flickered open.

"What?" he asked. He peered up at Colin. His hand darted out and fumbled for a pair of spectacles on his bedside table. The spectacles dropped to the floor when his fingers brushed against them. "Fucking hell, now look what you made me do. Who is it anyway?"

"It's me, Colin."

"What? Speak up, I can't hear you."

"For fuck's sake Dave, put your fucking hearing aid on. If I talk any louder The Gestapo will be back, wanting to see what's going on."

"What?"

Colin sighed and shook his head. He picked up Dave's hearing aid and hooked it over the man's ear. The hearing aid whistled while Dave sat up and fiddled with the volume control.

"I don't like this thing," Dave said, "it makes my tinnitus louder."

"That's because it's a cheap piece of fucking crap mate, same as everything else they give us in here."

"Is that you Colin? I can't see without my glasses."

"Yeah, mate."

"What's up?" Dave asked.

"I've had an idea."

"What about?"

"What we can do on Thatcher Day."

Dave rubbed his eyes and yawned. His elbows cracked when he stretched out his arms. "What the fuck time is it?" he asked.

"Never mind that. I've been reading the Thatcher Day posts on Silver Punkers, and you'll never guess who was on there."

"Sid Vicious?"

"Well yeah, there was quite a few of them. But I mean real people, not fucking nob-heads pretending to be some dead junkie. Only fucking Biffo Ratbastard. He were going on about this gig Sick Bastard did on the tenth anniversary on Parliament Square. Says they only got through two songs before the coppers smashed everything up and carted everyone off down to the cop-shop for a kicking. Anyway, that's what gave me the idea."

"Which is?" Dave asked.

Colin smiled. "I sent Biffo an entoMAIL asking what the chances are of Sick Bastard coming here to play live on Thatcher Day."

Dave shook his head. "Nah, The Gestapo would never allow that. Besides, it's probably not even the real Biffo Ratbastard, it'll just be someone pretending to be him."

"Nah, mate, it's deffo him. He's got a verified identity icon next to his avatar."

"Yeah well," Dave said, "even if it is really him, why would Sick Bastard want to come to a dump like this? Anyway, I thought they'd split up years ago. Didn't their drummer die or something?"

"Yeah, but look how many drummers they had, it was a different one on each album. They probably just got a new one."

"So what did Biffo have to say about it then?"

"Well he hasn't said nothing yet, I only sent the message a few minutes ago."

Dave sighed. "Fucking hell, so why wake me up then?"

"Because if Sick Bastard *do* come to play I'll need some help organising it, and there's not many other people here with a full set of marbles."

"Yeah well, until you hear from Biffo there's no point even talking about it, is there? I doubt he'd be interested anyway, someone like that. They were headlining the Blackpool Punk Festival for years, for fuck's sake, playing to massive crowds. Why would they want to come and play in a shitty retirement home in front of thirty coffin dodgers after that?" Dave took off his hearing aid, dropped it to the floor next to his spectacles, and lay down with his back to Colin.

Colin sighed and cracked his knuckles. He stood up with a grunt and went back to bed. He reached over to pick up his entoPAD from the bedside table and pulled a pair of headphones from a drawer. He prodded the entoPAD's screen to open entoTUNES, and swiped through the shortcuts to his favourite music. He settled down to listen to The Astronauts' It's All Done By Mirrors until he fell asleep and dreamed of being young.

* * *

Biffo Ratbastard sat in his ground floor flat, his bare feet up on a fluffy pink foot-rest, listening to Oi Polloi on his entoPAD. The music was fed to a pair of large wireless Jammo speakers placed either side of his armchair, and was cranked up so loud he couldn't hear his young upstairs neighbours banging on the ceiling. Not that it would have made any difference if he *could* hear them. What Biffo did on his own property was nothing to do with anyone else. Especially a bunch of snot-nosed students.

A half-empty can of Special Brew vibrated its way toward the edge of one of the speakers. Biffo reached out for it and took a long drink, draining the can. He crushed the can in his hand and tossed it at a round waste-bin in the corner of the room. The can hit the side of the bin and bounced off to join three more crushed cans on Biffo's thread-bare carpet.

"Bollocks," Biffo said, and took an electronic cigarette from his Motorhead dressing gown pocket. The end of the plastic cigarette glowed blue when he sucked on it. He exhaled the vapour with a sigh and closed his eyes as the nicotine rushed to his brain and mingled with the alcohol already swimming around in there.

Retirement life was fucking good, Biffo decided. He should have done it fifty years ago while he was still young enough to enjoy it.

Biffo was luckier than most people his age. He owned his own flat, and received regular monthly payments from entoCORP for his share of the advertising revenue each time one of his songs was streamed to a user's entoPAD. So when the government declared State Pension unsustainable due to advances in health care and an aging population, then abolished it completely along with all other state benefits, Biffo had managed to survive with his independence still intact.

He had to cut down on his fuel bills, wrapping himself up in thick clothes and blankets through the winter months instead of turning the heating on, and could only afford to drink Special Brew once a week by rationing the food he ate, but at least he hadn't been forced to move into one of the State Retirement Homes like so many of his generation. Death Homes, Biffo called them. Somewhere the government puts you out of the way, while they wait for you to die so they can seize whatever assets you've got left.

Biffo looked down at his entoPAD screen when one of Oi Polloi's Gaelic songs started playing. He prodded an icon in the corner of the screen and the lyrics were translated in real-time into Pidgin English that made no sense. Something about frogs dancing on a scientist's experience and systematic destruction of intercourse.

Biffo sighed and put the entoPAD down on the arm of his chair. He struggled to his feet and padded into the kitchen for another can of Special Brew. As he opened the fridge door Oi Polloi were cut off mid-song and replaced with a female robotic voice.

"You have new entoMAIL. You have new entoMAIL. You have new entoMAIL."

Biffo pulled out a can of Special Brew and cracked it open. Oi Polloi resumed from where they had left off. From the kitchen he could hear someone upstairs yell "Turn that fucking shit down!" Biffo took a long drink of Special Brew and belched, then returned to his armchair. He put the can down on top of a speaker and picked up his entoPAD. The screen flashed a message, *You have new entoMAIL.* Biffo prodded the entoMAIL icon and Oi Polloi were cut off once again, replaced with a video advert informing Biffo of the miracles of plastic hip replacements and how affordable they were with low monthly payments.

"Apply now and receive a free pen," a young woman in fishnet stockings and red suspender belt and bra said with a wink. "You know you want it."

The advert ended and Oi Polloi resumed playing. A text message displayed on the entoPAD screen, sandwiched between advertising banners extolling the joys of Viagra and live entoSEX, read:

All right mate, saw you on Silver Punkers and was wondering if you might be wanting to do something for Thatcher Day this year? 30 fucking years, can't believe it's been that long since the old witch snuffed it. Anyway, what do you reckon about Sick Bastard coming to play here or something? We can't afford to pay nothing, but there'd be free beer and stuff if you want?

The message was signed Punk76, and the sender used a red anarchy symbol as their avatar. Biffo Ratbastard shook his head and sighed. Why couldn't people use their real names? He could think of at least twelve people he knew who could have sent that message, and ticked off in his mind the ones who had died in the last few years. That left five possibles. Three if he discounted the ones with severe dementia.

Biffo read the message again and nodded to himself. Whoever it was from, the more he thought about it the more he liked the idea of being in front of an audience again. One last gig before he shuffles off forever, just like the last surviving member of the Sex Pistols did. There'd be no golden handshake, no million pound payout from entoCORP for the rights to record the gig for posterity. But free beer? Who could refuse an offer like that?

Biffo saved the message so he could reply to it later, and quit the entoMAIL app. He lowered the music's volume and heard a few thumps on the ceiling, followed by a cry of "About fucking time, you old bastard!"

"Fuck off," Biffo yelled, and opened the entoFACE app. He scrolled through his contacts and tapped on a photo of Steve Snitch. *Connecting*, the screen informed him. Biffo waited. And waited.

"This is Steve Snitch, leave a message and I might get back to you if I can be bothered. If you're just selling something, fuck off, I'm not interested."

Biffo sighed. "Snitchy, I'm thinking of getting the band back together. Let me know what you think when you hear this."

He returned to his contacts list and prodded Mike Hock's photo. Mike answered within a few seconds, and grinned out from the screen.

"All right Biffo, how's it fucking going?"

"Not bad mate, how's life treating you?"

"Can't complain. Well I can, but there's no point is there? No fucker cares."

"No, mate," Biffo said. "Anyway listen, I got a message from someone putting on a gig for Thatcher Day. What do you reckon about getting your bass out of storage and giving it another thrash for old time's sake?"

"Sounds good to me. Is Snitchy up for it?"

"Couldn't get hold of him, but I've left him a message."

"Yeah, he'll be tucked up in bed by now. You know they moved him into a retirement home?"

"No I didn't. Shit, when did that happen?"

"Fuck, it must be about six months ago now? He had to pay for emergency surgery and fell behind with his rent. They kicked him out and the rozzers picked him up sleeping rough and stuck him in a retirement home."

Biffo shook his head slowly and sighed. "Man, that's fucking bad news. I hope he's okay."

"Yeah he's fine," Mike said, nodding. "In fact he's fucking loving it. Says there's a few old Sick Bastard fans living there, he strums his guitar for them every night and they just lap it up."

"Good to hear. You kept up your playing too? Only we probably won't get much of a chance to practice before the gig."

"When is it?"

"Thatcher Day."

Mike laughed. "Just like old times, eh? It's not on fucking Parliament Square again, is it? I've still got the scars from that one."

"Yeah, me too. No, it's at one of the Death Homes. Not sure which one, I haven't confirmed it yet. Just wanted to sound you guys out first."

"Well I'm definitely in, and I'd be surprised if Snitchy wasn't too. You got a drummer lined up, or is it going to be an acoustic set? Old Vile would be a hard act to replace."

"Fuck acoustic sets, they're for dead hippies. I'd rather slit my fucking throat. We're a punk band, not a bunch of fucking Morris Dancers. You just leave finding a drummer to me and get practicing on that bass of yours. I'll send you the details when I've got them, and we'll get together somewhere for a practice."

"Look forward to it mate," Mike said. "Laters, then."

"Yeah. See you soon, Cocky."

Biffo quit entoFACE and cranked up the volume on the Oi Polloi song. He reached for his Special Brew and took a swig before opening the Silver Punkers Community Forum. Mike was right, Peter Vile would be hard to replace. He wasn't Sick Bastard's original drummer, but he was their longest running one and the best they had ever had. When he died five years ago, after contracting an infection following open-heart surgery, it had effectively ended the band's musical career. Drumming was a dying art, quite literally, with so many of the remaining punk bands having to resort to using electronic, computer-controlled drum machines instead.

Biffo composed a new message asking if anyone knew of any drummers in the Shefferham area who would be available to play on Thatcher Day. Own kit essential. Experience, don't give a fuck either way.

He drained the rest of his Special Brew and threw the can at the waste-bin. This time he hit it dead-centre and the can dropped in with a clatter.

* * *

Colin Baxter leaned against a ten-foot high wooden gate built into an even higher, barbed-wire topped wall surrounding the retirement home's concrete yard. He looked longingly at the French doors leading back into the communal lounge; but they weren't due to be reopened for at least another twenty minutes, after the cleaning staff finished their weekly routine. He shivered and blew on his hands to warm them, then thrust them deep into his dressing gown pockets.

The retirement home manager looked down from an upstairs window. The thumping, screeching wail of trippy technobabble music drifted through the open window, grating on Colin's nerves. Colin didn't see the point of music like that. It was just noise as far as he was concerned. The singer wasn't even shouting.

Dave Turner and Louise Brown were kicking a large inflatable beach-ball across the yard to each other. Frank Sterner hobbled between them, getting in the way. The ball bounced off Frank's walking frame and veered off course toward Colin. Colin leaned on his walking stick and kicked it back to Louise once Frank was out of the way.

Other than Frank's endless wanderings, Dave and Louise were the only people active in the back yard. Everyone else stood around like wrinkled zombies that had been left in the bath too long, just waiting until they could return to the warmth of the retirement home lounge. Several pairs of eyes peered through the window, watching the cleaning staff turn their world upside down in the pursuit of cleanliness. Chairs were up-ended, biscuit crumbs sucked from every crevice by droning deep-cleaners. Even all the posters and framed copies of old record sleeves and punk fanzines were taken down from the walls and polished to gleaming perfection.

"Oi Colin," Dave shouted as he kicked the beach-ball to

Louise. "You heard anything from that Biffo yet?"

Colin shook his head. "Nah, mate. Looks like you were right, he's not interested."

"That's a shame," Dave said.

"Yeah. Not to worry though, I'll think of something else we can do to mark the occasion. Even if we have to set up the fucking karaoke machine and have a sing-song. There's loads of Thatcher songs from the 80s we could do."

Dave walked over and leaned against the gate by Colin's side. "Yeah, that'd be good. We could get Old Frank to do Walk On By." Colin laughed. "Stranglers version, of course. You know how he doesn't like anything recorded after 1979."

"Yeah, I never did understand that bollocks myself."

"What bollocks is that then?" Louise asked, joining them.

"That fucking 'punk died in 1979' bollocks. I were still a kid at school back then, so it didn't even start for me until the 1980s."

Louise nodded. "Yeah, me too."

"I were sixteen in 1976, just the right age," Dave said with a smile. "I saw the Sex Pistols twice, you know. Once with Matlock, the other with Vicious. My brother, he were a few years older than me, like, he used to sneak me into the local punk nightclub. Saw fucking loads of bands there, I did. Vibrators, Lurkers, The Adverts, X-Ray Spex, even the fucking Clash played there once."

"Jammy bastard," Colin said. "I didn't get to see the Sex Pistols until 1996 when they were all old and fat. Still fucking great though."

"Yeah," Dave agreed. "Shame about old Johnny Rotten though." He laughed. "I remember one time after his

Country Life butter thing, we went to see Public Image Ltd and there were these blokes throwing blocks of fucking butter at him. Took the wrappers off first, of course. Old Johnny had a right fit about it, said if they didn't pack it in he was going home."

"Never cared much for PIL," Colin said. "The first single was okay, but everything else I heard by them I thought it were shite. The 80s bands were loads better. Exploited, Vice Squad, The Enemy, Abrasive Wheels, Mau Maus, Cockney Upstarts, Blitz, fucking loads of great bands came out in the 80s. That's why Old Frank's full of shit. Most of them were even on Top of the fucking Pops too, so how could punk be dead in 1979?"

"Don't forget Crass," Louise said.

"Yeah well," Colin said, "I never really cared much for them either. There were a gang of Crass Punks used hang out on our council estate, they were always giving us stick about Wattie from The Exploited being an ex-soldier. As if that fucking mattered. Supposed to be all about anarchy and peace, but that didn't stop them from sticking the boot into anyone wearing an Exploited T-shirt."

"I just liked their music," Louise said, "never got into the politics part myself. Except when this bunch of fucking Nazis turned up at one of their gigs and started pushing everyone around." She spat on the ground. "Fucking Nazis."

"Yeah," Colin said. "Cockney Upstarts used to attract them too. My mate Bri got stabbed at one of their gigs, put me off seeing them again for life. I couldn't even bring myself to play their records again for years after that."

Colin looked across at the French doors when he heard them open. The residents shuffled back inside and slumped into their armchairs, picked up their entoPADs. Colin nodded at Louise, who shrugged at Dave, and the three of them made their way inside. Louise plugged the speakers back in and The Sex Pistols began playing mid-song, drowning out the manager's trippy technobabble from upstairs.

Colin sat down and picked up his entoPAD. *You have new entoMAIL*, the screen informed him. The screen was smeared with waxy furniture polish, and Colin wiped it off with a corner of his dressing gown. He prodded the entoMAIL icon and sat through an advert for hair transplants while he waited for the message to display:

Re Thatcher Day. Yeah mate, sounds good. That fucking bitch destroyed my home town, so it deserves celebrating in style. Give us the venue and time and we'll be there to rock your fucking heads off. Biffo Ratbastard.

Colin smiled. He turned to Dave to tell him the good news, but Dave had fallen asleep. Bursting to tell someone, Colin looked across the lounge at Louise Brown. She sat with her entoPAD on her lap, the palms of both hands drumming along with Paul Cook on the arms of her chair. Her head bobbed, and she sang along tunelessly to Bodies. Colin waved her over but she didn't see him, lost in her own little world.

Still in entoMAIL, Colin composed a message to Louise asking her to meet him by the games table. He put down his entoPAD and sat back to watch her reaction. Louise stopped drumming and picked up her entoPAD. She frowned at whatever advert she was subjected to, then looked up at Colin and smiled. She raised a bony thumb in Colin's direction and pushed herself upright using the arms of her chair. Colin struggled upright himself, and made his way to the games table. He took his entoPAD with him and placed it down on the table's glass surface. He sat down on one of the padded stools placed around the table just as Louise arrived.

"What's up?" she asked, sliding into a seat opposite

Colin. She swiped her hand across the table's surface, scrolling through the selection of games available.

"Do you remember Sick Bastard?"

"Yeah, of course I fucking do," Louise said. "Do you remember how to play Tic-Tac-Toe?" she added, sarcastically. Colin nodded. "Right then, I'll play you for a biscuit. Deal?"

Colin nodded. "Yeah, okay. But have a look at this first."

Colin slid his entoPAD across the table. Louise looked down at it. Her lips moved as she read, and when she came to the end of the message she looked up at Colin. The wrinkles in her face turned into deep crevices as she cracked a wide smile.

"No fucking way," she said. "Biffo Ratbastard? I didn't even know he was still alive, I thought he had a heart attack a few years ago."

"No, that was their drummer," Colin said.

"And he's coming here?"

Colin smiled. "Looks like it, yeah."

"I fucked him once, you know," Louise said with smile. She looked down at the games table and prodded the centre square of a Tic-Tac-Toe grid, planting an X in it. "Back in the day obviously, not recently. I would've been about seventeen, he wasn't much older himself. It was before they were famous, they were just a local band back then. Me and my mate Tracey got chatting with them at the bar after a gig, then I ended up in the back of Biffo's transit van in the car park. Tracey had a knee-trembler in the blokes' bogs with the guitarist, can't remember his name, but she said he were a right dirty cunt when I met up with her later. Biffo were sweet as fuck. He even gave me his phone number, but I never called it."

"How come?" Colin asked. He prodded the middle-left

square of the Tic-Tac-Toe board.

Louise shrugged and prodded the top-right. "Never really got round to it. Besides, he weren't nothing back then, just your average bloke in a band playing back-street pubs and going nowhere. If I'd known back then he was going to be famous one day, maybe I would've called him, kept in touch."

"Maybe he'll remember you?"

Louise laughed. "I doubt it. He'll have had a girl in every town, probably a whole fucking queue of them after they started headlining. I'd be just one of thousands. So how are you planning to get Sick Bastard past The Gestapo then?"

"I don't know yet," Colin said. "I didn't really think they'd come so I didn't plan that far ahead. But I'll think of something. I'll need to get hold of some beer too, I said that's what they'll get paid with."

Louise smiled. "Good luck with that one. Nobody's managed to smuggle beer into this shit-hole since I've been here. But if you do somehow manage it, get me some too, yeah? I haven't had a good piss up in donkeys' years."

"Yeah, no worries," Colin said, nodding. "Have you, um, got any money you can chip in toward the cost? I've only got thirty quid and that won't get us much."

Louise sighed and shook her head slowly. "Well that's twenty more than me, I'm fucking skint. I tell you who will have some money, though."

"Who's that?" Colin asked.

Louise turned and nodded at Greg Lomax. "Old Greg over there. He's fucking loaded."

Colin smiled. "Yeah, right," he said, sarcastically.

"No, straight up. Before his stroke he used to be a fucking novelist, would you believe? Remember all those punk and skinhead books Hool-ePress brought out? He wrote some of those. Cracking reads they were, too. I was dead impressed when he told me, I used to love those books."

Colin looked at Greg Lomax in wonder.

"Your move," Louise said.

Colin looked down at the Tic-Tac-Toe board and prodded a vacant square. "So how come I never heard of him then? I read some of those books too, but I don't remember his name being on any of them."

"He used a fucking pseudonym, didn't he? You know, for tax and shit, probably. Now what did he call himself?" Louise frowned, deep in concentration. "Shit, he did tell me the name, but I can't fucking remember. Mark something, maybe? Or it could have been Blake, I don't know. Anyway, entoCORP owns all the rights now, same as everything else, so they'll be on entoBOOKS if you want to have a look at them. He gets a dollar for every ten pages someone reads, double that much if they respond to one of the adverts and buy something. He's fucking minted, he showed me his entoBANK summary once and there was like thousands and thousands in it. Fuck knows why he moved in here, he could've easily afforded to live somewhere decent instead."

"You reckon he'd chip in for the beer?" Colin asked.

"Dunno, maybe. It's not like he's got anything else to spend his money on, is it? Leave it with me, I'll sort Greg out. You order the beer and figure out some way of getting it through the door." She prodded the Tic-Tac-Toe board and pushed herself to her feet. "My game," she said, and walked away. "That's a biscuit you owe me," she called out over her shoulder.

Colin looked down at his entoPAD. He composed a message to Biffo Ratbastard, telling him the gig was at State

Retirement Home SY-379 at seven pm on the evening of Thatcher Day.

Now all he had to do was figure out how to get both the band, and the beer, past The Gestapo and whichever workfare assistant was working that day.

* * *

"Yeah?" Biffo Ratbastard said, peering at a bald, wrinkled face filling the screen of his entoPAD. The man's wide, staring, blood-shot eyes darted around, as if he could see straight through Biffo and was taking in his surroundings. A deep, Z-shaped scar like the mark of Zorro ran down the left side of his face, starting just below his eye and ending at the corner of his mouth.

"Is that Biffo Ratbastard?" the man asked.

"Yeah?"

"Someone said you was looking for a drummer."

"Yeah, I am. You got your own kit then?"

"Yeah. I haven't got no transport though, so you'd have to pick me up."

"No problem," Biffo said, "I'm still mobile. You been playing long?"

The man smiled, revealing a row of crooked yellow teeth. "What, you don't recognise me?"

Biffo tried to remember the name of the caller entoFACE had prompted him with just before he accepted the connection. Simon something-or-other, but it hadn't been a name he recognised.

"What's your name, mate?" Biffo asked.

"You'd probably know me as Fungal Matters."

Biffo leaned forward in his chair and moved the

entoPAD closer to his face to get a better look. Fungal Matters! Now there was a name Biffo hadn't heard for a long time. Fungal had drummed with some of the top punk bands of the early twenty-first century, but had disappeared without trace in 2020. There had been a lot of online speculation about what had happened to him; some said he had gone to live in a tepee in the woods and survived on a diet of wild squirrels, while others said he was working as a car mechanic in Barnsley. Some even said he had become a property tycoon in New York, investing heavily in wind-farms and student accommodation.

Biffo tried to picture the man as he would have looked twenty-five years ago, when he was in his early fifties, a couple of years before his disappearance. Sick Bastard had headlined a punk festival in Brighton, with Fungal's band at the time Underclass Strike Back supporting. They had shared an after-gig joint together to wind down in the venue's dressing room before making their separate ways.

Fungal had aged badly. His trademark green and red double-mohican was gone, replaced with liver-spots and pock-marks covering his entire head. His eyes were hollow, sunk deep into his face, and never ceased their endless wandering. His nose was crooked, and looked like it had been broken several times. A long, white goatee beard was braided into five individual strands, with red and black alternating beads threaded onto each strand. They hung from his chin like crusty stalactites and clicked together when he moved his head.

"You still there?" Fungal asked.

"Yeah mate," Biffo said, nodding. He took out his electronic cigarette and popped it in his mouth, sat back in his chair. "Fungal Matters, fucking hell. It's been a fucking long time, mate. Where have you been hiding?"

"Hiding?"

"Yeah, mate. You just seemed to fucking vanish one day. Where did you go?"

"Nowhere, why?"

Biffo took a deep drag on his electronic cigarette and sighed as he exhaled. "Mate, you were one of the big fucking mysteries of the day. Every fucker and his dog had a theory about what happened to you."

"Well all they had to do was ask me," Fungal said with a shrug.

Biffo smiled and shook his head. "Fucking hell. So you kept up with the drumming then?"

"Yeah. Well, no, not really. But I took it up again a few years ago and I've still got my old kit."

"Do you know any of our songs?"

"Sick Bastard? Yeah, of course I fucking do. I listen to them all the time on entoTUNES."

Biffo's eyes widened. "Really? Wow, that's great, Fungal. So are you free on Thatcher Day? I know it's a bit short notice."

"Yeah, I'm free all the time. You'd need to pick me up though. I've got no transport."

"Where are you living these days?"

"Scunthorpe."

"Shouldn't be a problem. Give me your address and I'll come down mid-week with the rest of the band, we can have a bit of a practice jam."

* * *

Biffo climbed out of his electric transit van and walked through a metal gate leading to a dilapidated-looking mid-terrace house. Net curtains twitched in the window of the house next door. Biffo heard the van door slam, then Mike Hock joined him at the door with a bass guitar slung over his shoulder. Biffo rapped on the door with his knuckles. A dog inside the house barked once, and the door opened a few minutes later.

"Yeah?" Fungal Matters said, looking out. His eyes swivelled in all directions. The dog, a black Labrador, stood by his side. A harness around the dog's neck led to a plastic handle, which Fungal held in one hand.

"It's us, mate," Biffo said. He tapped his chest. "Sick Bastard. We've come down for a practice session."

"Oh right," Fungal said, smiling. "Come in, then. My drums are through here."

Fungal stood to one side and gestured at a room to one side of the hallway. The dog sniffed Biffo's hand. Biffo bent down and patted the dog's head, then squeezed past Fungal and entered the room. It was dark and gloomy, the curtains drawn. A table with one chair stood in one corner of the room, a large black leather settee lined the wall under the window. Fungal's drums stood in the opposite corner to the table, a small wooden stool behind them. There were no posters or photographs on the walls, no ornaments on display anywhere in the room. The faded, skull-patterned wallpaper looked like it had hung there for decades, and cobwebs hung down from the yellowed ceiling.

"Take a seat, I'll go get some beers," Fungal said from the hallway.

Biffo sat down on the leather settee and Mike propped his bass guitar up against the table.

"I'll go get my practice amp from the van," Mike said. Biffo tossed him the keys and Mike caught them in one hand before leaving.

Fungal returned clutching four glass beer bottles by

their stems, with a bottle opener hooked over his thumb. He put the bottles down on the table and released the dog's harness. The dog bounded onto the settee and lay down next to Biffo. It watched him with its head resting on its front paws. Fungal felt along the stem of a beer bottle with one hand and placed the bottle opener over it. The bottle opened with a hiss and he held it out in one hand.

"Cheers mate," Biffo said. He leaned forward and took the bottle. He looked at the label and took a sip while Fungal opened another bottle. "Good choice in beer, mate. Who's the other one for?"

"Oh," Fungal said, "is there not three of you? I thought you said you were bringing the rest of the band down for a practice."

Mike returned with his practice amp and placed it down in the centre of the room. He plugged it into a wall socket and looked at the beer bottles on the table. He picked one up and opened it. "Just the fucking job, cheers," he said, and took a long drink.

"I were going to," Biffo said, looking up at Fungal, "but I couldn't spring old Snitchy from the Gulag they've got him in. They said I need to fill a form in at least three days in advance if I want to take him out anywhere. Fucking health and safety or some such bollocks, they said. Fucking daft if you ask me, but I'll get it sorted in time for the gig on Thatcher Day. Meanwhile I've got him on my entoPAD, I'll hook it up to Mike's amp and he can play through that. It's the best I could do, really."

"Oh, okay," Fungal said. "You do that while I warm up."

Fungal took a bottle of beer from the table and made his way to the drum kit in the corner of the room. Halfway there he stubbed his toe against Mike's practice amp and cried out in surprise.

"What's that?"

He raised his hands and waved them in the air before him, as if he were searching for an invisible barrier he had stumbled into.

"It's my amp," Mike said. He walked up to Fungal and waved his hand in front of the man's face. "You can't see, can you?"

"No," Fungal said. "That's why I need to know where everything is." He skirted around Mike's amp and resumed walking to his drum kit, suddenly more cautious.

"What happened to your sight, mate?" Biffo asked.

"Cataracts."

"Cataracts? I thought they could be cured?"

"Yeah well, they can if you can afford the fucking treatment. I tried to get a loan to pay for it but they said I was a bad payment risk and turned me down. Apparently royalty payments from entoCORP aren't classed as regular income."

"Fucking cunts," Biffo said. He shook his head. "That's fucking terrible."

"It's not so bad," Fungal said. He sat down on the stool behind his drum kit and picked up his sticks. "You get used to it after a while, and I've got Gristle over there to help me get about."

The dog's ears pricked up on hearing its name, and it looked over at Fungal. Fungal tapped his drum sticks together and beat them against each of his drums in turn. He started slow, then built up speed, ending with a drum-roll and a clash of cymbals.

Biffo stood up with a grunt. "Might as well get fucking started then," he said. He propped his entoPAD up against a beer bottle on top of Mike's practice amp and plugged a cable into its headphone socket. "You ready, Snitchy?"

On the entoPAD screen, dressed in black and red pyjamas, Steve Snitch sat in an armchair. On his knee lay a pink, leopard-pattern guitar, the fretboard propped up against an arm of the chair. Steve raised a gnarled thumb and said "Yeah." His voice came from the practice amp.

"Cheers Snitchy," Biffo said. He raised a beer bottle to the entoPAD screen in a toast.

"Fuck off, you cunt," Steve said, smiling. "I hope it fucking chokes you."

Mike strapped on his bass guitar and plugged it into the amp. He strummed along with Steve Snitch while he twiddled volume controls on top of the amp to get a good balance, slightly favouring his own bass over Steve's lead guitar.

Biffo sat down next to Fungal's dog. "Right then, let's fucking do this. We'll try State Pension first, yeah?" He looked at Mike, who nodded. Steve, on the entoPAD screen, raised his thumb again. "One, two, three, four –" Biffo shouted.

A cacophonous sound erupted from the small practice amp. The dog barked and ran from the room. Biffo waited for his cue and snarled the opening lines.

"We don't give a fuck about your years of austerity, we just want to fucking party. You sit there in your Westminster bubble, well here's some old cunts who'll give you some trouble."

Listening to the band play sent a cold shiver down Biffo's spine. They sounded good, he thought, and took another sip of beer while he waited for his next cue. Fungal's drumming was a bit off, he was a lot slower than Biffo would like and he skipped a few of the more intricate beats that were Peter Vile's speciality. Mike Hock's bass was a bit rusty too, but Steve Snitch's guitar work was spot on. The others would get there in the end, Biffo was sure of it. A few solid hours of practice and they would all be ready for the gig on Thatcher Day.

* * *

On the morning of Thatcher Day, Colin Baxter woke with a dawn chorus of chirping birds and the early morning sun streaming through the open dormitory window. He sat up in bed and stretched, slid back the bedcover and directed his feet into his Sex Pistols slippers. He hobbled from bed to bed, rousing the occupants with a gentle poke from his walking stick.

"Wake up, you lazy bastards, it's Thatcher Day."

"Fuck off," Frank Sterner mumbled. He rolled over and pulled the covers over his head.

"Come on you cunts, wake up," Colin said. "It's the best fucking day of the year, and I don't want to waste a second of it. We need to get the decorations up in the lounge, then we can start the party proper." Colin stood in the middle of the dormitory, looking at each bed in turn. Nobody roused. "Fucking hell, you lazy bastards," he said, shaking his head.

Colin walked back to his bed and picked up his entoPAD from the bedside table. He swiped the screen to wake the device up, then went into its configuration settings to switch sound output to the built in speakers. He set the volume to maximum, opened entoTUNES, and scrolled down to find the song he wanted.

Sick Bastard's Ding Dong the Bitch is Fucking Dead, a re-working of an old song from The Wizard of Oz, blasted out from the entoPAD's speakers. Old men all around Colin groaned and complained at the sudden noise. One swore. Another sat up and threw a pillow at Colin. Colin smiled and set the song on repeat, not prepared to give anyone a chance to drift off back to sleep.

After a few plays of Ding Dong the Bitch is Fucking Dead, the dormitory door slammed open and the retirement home manager glared in at Colin. His eyes were red and puffy, his hair a mess. He wore a silk dressing gown with a dragon printed on it, and his feet were bare.

"Turn that noise off and get back into bed, Baxter!" he shouted from the doorway.

Colin turned his back on the man and shouted along with the song's chorus. The loud music, in combination with the noise both he and the manager were making, started to have its desired effect. Men sat up in bed and scratched themselves, looked around bleary-eyed and yawned. Some reached out for false teeth or spectacles from their bedside tables. Only Dave Turner, oblivious to everything without his hearing aid, snored on.

The manager stamped over to Colin and snatched the entoPAD from his hand. "I said turn that noise off!" He prodded the screen angrily, and tossed the device onto Colin's bed.

"Oi you cunt, I were listening to that," Colin yelled.

The manager shrugged. "Yeah well you're not now. People are trying to sleep, so you'd better get back into bed and join them or else."

"Happy Thatcher Day to you too," Colin said with a sneer. He turned away and reached for his entoPAD, to check it wasn't damaged.

The manager laughed, humourlessly. "What is it with you people and Thatcher? She's been dead and gone thirty years now, and it's even longer since she was in power. So don't you think it's time you got over it?"

Colin wheeled back to the manager and raised his walking stick. He shook it. "You what? That fucking bitch destroyed Yorkshire. I don't care how long it's been, I'll never forgive her for that."

"Destroyed Yorkshire my arse," the manager said. He grabbed the end of Colin's walking stick and used it to push him back against the bed. "That's not what they taught us in history. It was that Scargill and his militants wanting to hold the country to ransom. Thatcher just gave them a slap to put them in their place." Colin tried to wrestle back his walking stick, but the manager held it tight. "They were just commies," the manager continued, "and they got what they deserved. Anyway, I don't care and this isn't up for discussion. You either get back into bed right now or there isn't going to be a Thatcher Day for any of you. Your choice."

Colin glared at the manager and tried again to wrestle his walking stick free. As Colin tugged at one end, the manager pushed at the other. Colin fell down hard to a sitting position on the bed and cried out at a stabbing pain in his knee. The walking stick slipped from his fingers. He clutched his knee and turned to the manager, ready to call him a cunt for what he had just done.

The manager held Colin's walking stick above his head, ready to strike at any moment.

Colin cried out in alarm. He raised his hands to cover his face. He trembled in anticipation of the punishment to come. He heard someone gasp, someone else implore the manager not to do it, but he didn't dare look to see who it was. After a short pause, when no blow came, Colin spread his fingers and peeked through them. The walking stick wavered in the air before him, the manager still glaring down at him.

"You've got ten seconds to get back in that bed," the manager said. Colin lay down and pulled the bedcover over his head. "Wise choice." Colin jumped when he heard the walking stick clatter down by the side of the bed. "Same goes for the rest of you. If I hear any more noise from any of you before breakfast, that's it. No Thatcher Day for any of you." The door slammed.

"You all right, Colin?" Frank Sterner whispered.

Colin pushed back the bed cover and reached for his entoPAD. "Yeah. Fucking cunt. He's got a big surprise coming if he thinks he can do us out of our Thatcher Day party this year."

"You'd best not wind him up too much, you know what he can be like sometimes."

Colin propped himself up against a pillow and prodded the Silver Punkers Community Forum icon on his entoPAD. The Thatcher Day 30 thread he was following had an additional nine hundred and sixty-one new posts since he had looked the previous night. He settled down to read them while everyone else drifted off back to sleep.

* * *

Breakfast was the usual watery porridge the residents were served every morning, and Colin slurped it up from a red plastic bowl while The Ruts played quietly in the background. He drank the porridge fast, eager to make a start on the Thatcher Day decorations. He put down the bowl and wiped dribbles from his chin with the palm of his hand, then wiped his hand down the side of his Exploited T-shirt.

Louise Brown, sitting opposite Colin, rested her elbows on the table while she too finished off her morning porridge. She wore a faded, moth-eaten Vice Squad T-shirt beneath a pink mohair cardigan, but it was Louise's hair that took centre stage in Colin's attention. Before leaving the women's dormitory for breakfast Louise had dyed her hair blue and spiked it up. Colin looked down at the image printed on Louise's T-shirt. The resemblance between Louise and the very young Beki Bondage was striking. They could almost be grandmother and granddaughter.

Louise leaned forward to put her porridge bowl down on the table. Colin caught a quick glimpse of multi-coloured tattoos through the holes in her T-shirt. He wondered what they were, and whether Louise would show him if he asked. Louise coughed theatrically. Colin looked up. She frowned.

"I like your hair like that," Colin said. "You should do it like that more often."

Louise smiled. "Thank you. You can use some of my hair wax if you want to do yours?"

Colin raised a hand to his temple and twisted strands of white hair between his fingers. "Yeah that'd be great, thanks. Have you got any blue dye going spare too?"

Louise shook her head. "No, sorry. I could only afford a small bottle, I used it all up this morning."

"Oh well. I'll just have to go natural then."

A workfare assistant took their bowls away and Louise slid her chair back, leaned on the table, and stood up. She pulled her black PVC mini-skirt down to cover her thighs, and turned away. Colin stared at Louise's ragged fishnet stockings while she walked to her armchair and sat down. She picked up her entoPAD and looked down at the screen.

Colin leaned on his walking stick and stood up when The Ruts were replaced with X-Ray Spex. He hobbled over to the speakers and turned up the volume, sang along with Poly Styrene. The song reminded Colin again of the Woolworths security guard he used to have so much fun with when he was young. He wondered if the man had still been working there when Woolworths closed down, whether he had ever found another job.

The workfare assistant glared at Colin and resumed

clearing away the breakfast things. He shooed the last of the stragglers away from the dining table and folded its sides down, pushed it against a wall out of the way.

Louise put down her entoPAD and joined Colin by the speakers. "Come on then," she said, and took Colin by the hand.

She led him out of the communal lounge and into the women's dormitory. She sat him down on the edge of her bed and took a tub of hair wax from a drawer in her bedside cabinet. She scooped out a handful of wax and smeared it over the strands of hair on Colin's right temple, then stretched it out sideways, sandwiching his hair between the palms of her hands. She stood back, admiring her handiwork, and scraped excess wax from her hands back into the tub. Colin raised his hand to feel for himself what she had done with his hair.

"Give it a few minutes to harden before you touch it," Louise warned. She took a hand-mirror from the drawer and held it out.

Colin looked at the side-mohican Louse had moulded his hair into and frowned. He had never joined the mohican tribe when he was young. Even when just about everyone he knew started sprouting them he had preferred to keep the classic punk look. He combed his fingers through the mohican, separated it into five sections, and twisted each section into a spike.

"That's better," Colin said, nodding to the mirror. He smiled at Louise. "Come on, then. Let's go put the decorations up."

Back in the lounge, Frank Sterner shuffled around the room with his walking frame. Colin skirted around him and woke up Dave Turner, who had drifted off to sleep despite the loud music. Together with Louise, they raided a store-cupboard in the hallway and pulled out a large cardboard box. Inside were balloons and banners, party hats and streamers. They carried the box into the lounge between them and put it down between the speakers.

Louise unrolled a black canvas banner with white skulls printed at each end, and stencilled block-capital text between them reading DING DONG THE WITCH IS DEAD. She climbed onto her armchair and attached one end of the banner to the wall behind it with Blu-tack. She climbed down and picked up the other end of the banner, stretched it out to where Fiona Scott sat, and climbed up beside her. Fiona shuffled to one side to make room for Louise, and turned around to watch. Fiona's eyes lit up when she saw the banner, reflecting a hint of interest usually absent from her. The faint trace of a smile appeared on her face.

Dave Turner unfolded a large Spitting Image poster of Thatcher with the words DEAD DEAD DEAD scrawled on her forehead in red marker pen. He stretched up and fastened the poster to the wall at a crooked angle. Frank Sterner wandered over to have a look, mumbled "Fucking bitch," and walked away.

Colin took a handful of black balloons from the box and showed them to Tony Harris. Tony nodded, and pulled the plastic tube from his face-mask. Colin stretched a balloon over the end of the tube and held it tight while he twisted a dial on Tony's oxygen cylinder. The balloon inflated, displaying the phrase I STILL FUCKING HATE THATCHER. Colin tied off the end of the balloon, batted it away from him, and attached another.

With all the balloons inflated, Colin re-attached the tube to Tony's face-mask and left the communal lounge. He walked up the corridor to the men's dormitory and made for a large wardrobe they all shared. He pulled out a dusty cardboard box from the bottom of the wardrobe, set it down on a nearby bed, ripped brown parcel tape from the top of the box, and lifted the flaps.

Thatcher stared out at him from the box. Her wide, blood-shot eyes seemed to bore straight into his soul. A disturbed spider ran across Thatcher's long, pointy nose and disappeared into her gaping red mouth.

A cold shiver ran down Colin's spine.

He reached down and curled his fingers around Thatcher's nose. Her withered, naked body unfurled before him with a slight crackling sound as Colin pulled her out of the box. He felt an intense rage and punched her in the face.

"Fucking bitch," he shouted, and threw her onto the bed.

The spider darted from Thatcher's mouth and ran across the bed in search of a new hiding place. Colin squeezed his hands around Thatcher's neck. Thatcher stared up at him, as uncaring as she had ever been. Colin lifted her from the bed and shook her. A cloud of dust made him sneeze. He shook her again, swiped cobwebs from Thatcher's sagging breasts with one hand. He dragged her back to the lounge by the neck.

Colin paused in the lounge doorway and looked in. Billy Bragg sang about waiting for the great leap forwards while a few people batted balloons to each other and sang along with him. Louise Brown twirled her arms around slowly as she danced before one of the speakers.

"Oi Tony, look who's here," Colin called out. He held Thatcher before him and shook her.

Tony Harris smiled when he turned to look. He struggled to his feet and limped toward Colin, pushing a trolley containing his oxygen cylinder before him.

Colin squeezed one of Thatcher's breasts and put the nipple to his mouth. He bit down on it, prised open a valve with his teeth, and attached it to Tony's oxygen cylinder tube. Thatcher's body crackled as it took shape. Twisted arms uncurled themselves and reached out like a hungry zombie. Her legs straightened and ballooned out, supporting her on huge, webbed feet.

When she was fully formed, Colin squeezed Thatcher's nipple between his thumb and forefinger and pulled the plastic tube free. Oxygen hissed from the tube while he handed it back to Tony. Tony re-attached the tube to his face mask while Colin wrestled Thatcher's nipple valve closed.

Colin squeezed each of Thatcher's arms and legs in turn to check for any punctures left from the previous year's Thatcher Day celebrations. Satisfied she was uninjured, he gripped her by the neck and held her out before him while he hobbled through the doorway into the lounge.

"Where there is hope, let us bring despair," Colin said in a high-pitched, screeching voice. "Where there is prosperity, let us bring poverty. Bring me the head of Arthur Scargill, for I have returned from hell to give you an eternity of torment."

Fiona Scott looked up and gasped, raised a hand to her mouth in shock. Frank Sterner, who had been shuffling across the room, veered off course and inched toward Colin with a look of pure hatred on his face.

"You fucking evil bitch," Frank yelled. He shook with rage, his knuckles white around the top of the walking frame. He hacked up and spat in Thatcher's face. Thatcher stared back defiantly while thick brown mucus dribbled down her cheek.

"How very dare you, you ignorant fucking Yorkshire pleb," Colin screeched. He swatted Frank with one of Thatcher's outstretched hands.

Dave Turner walked over and punched Thatcher in the stomach with such ferocity it made Colin stumble back a few steps. Colin steadied himself with his walking stick and swung Thatcher down to headbutt Dave, but the old man was ready and punched her in the face long before she made impact.

Soon Colin was surrounded by a mob of angry geriatrics shouting abuse at Thatcher, and was forced to drop her and move out of the way for his own safety as they set about her with fists and walking sticks. Even Greg Lomax joined in, his eyes blazing, his body trembling with rage as he kicked out at her.

The workfare assistant watched in wide-eyed disbelief. "Settle down now, you lot," he shouted, stepping toward the melee around Thatcher, "before you do yourselves a mischief."

Dave Turner stamped on Thatcher's crotch and her upper body reared up like a vampire rising from its coffin. Fiona Scott screamed and fainted backwards. The workfare assistant caught her by the armpits and lowered her to the floor. He dragged her away, shaking his head.

The attack on Thatcher lasted several minutes until the last of the retirement home residents finished venting their rage. Thatcher stared up at them as they wheezed and panted for breath around her.

"Thatcher's dead," Colin shouted. He raised his walking stick above his head. "Happy Thatcher Day, everyone."

There were panted responses of "Happy Thatcher Day" from those who had recovered their breath. Others just smiled and nodded their heads. Dave Turner reached behind one of the speakers and pulled out a cable, silencing The Vibrators mid-song with a loud electrical pop. He plugged his entoPAD into the speakers, and Sick Bastard's Ding Dong the Fucking Bitch is Dead blasted out.

Colin nodded in approval at Dave's choice of music and joined in with the spontaneous dancing that broke out. At the song's chorus everyone stopped gyrating as one and pointed down at Thatcher's corpse while they shouted along with Biffo Ratbastard's vocals – "You're dead, you're dead, you're fucking dead!" – then resumed dancing.

It wasn't long before people started to drift away, exhausted and red faced, back to their armchairs. Only Colin Baxter and Louise Brown remained by the speakers. Colin leaned on his walking stick and jerked his shoulders while Louise's slippered feet shuffled across the carpet to the sound of The Exploited's Maggie You Cunt. It was one of the band's later, thrash-tempo releases from the mid-1990s, and Colin wished he still had the energy to keep up with its fast beat.

He shouted along with Wattie at the chorus, "Maggie Maggie Maggie Maggie, you fucking cunt!"

If Colin was honest he would admit those were the only words he could decipher from Wattie's thick Scottish accent. Louise, meanwhile, seemed to know every word.

The song ended and Steve Ignorant shouted "How does it feel?" Colin's shoulders slumped and he panted for breath. Sweat poured down from his armpits, sticking his T-shirt to his body. Louise continued dancing by his side, her fist punching the air in delight as she sang along with the Crass song. She stopped when she noticed Colin standing motionless beside her, and frowned at him.

"You pegging out on me too?" she shouted, hands on hips.

"No, I just don't like Crass," Colin shouted back. "I *am* fucking knackered though. And we should save some energy for when Sick Bastard gets here."

Louise laughed. "You fucking lightweight. You're eighty, not a hundred and fifty. There's plenty of time for resting when you're dead, so come on, get fucking dancing."

Oi Polloi's Fuck Everybody Who Voted Tory started up and Louise raised her arms and twirled like an arthritic ballerina to the slow beats of the opening monologue. When the song sped up and got going proper, she flailed her arms wildly and lurched toward Colin. She bumped into him, causing him to drop his walking stick and stumble to one side. Colin grabbed onto Louise's mohair cardigan with both hands to steady himself and she stumbled with him, laughing as they both fell to their knees. She stopped laughing when she saw the pain on Colin's face.

"Sorry," she shouted. "I didn't mean to do that, I just got a bit carried away."

Colin clutched his knee and grimaced. "It's okay. Can you pass me my walking stick? I can't get up without it."

Louise crawled over to where Colin's walking stick lay and slid it across the carpet toward him. She shuffled herself onto her bottom and sat back, leaning on her hands. She twitched her feet and nodded her head in time to the music while Colin struggled to his feet. Colin leaned on his walking stick and panted. He looked down at Louise.

Louise smiled up and raised her hands out to Colin, like a small child wanting to be picked up. "Guess what?" she shouted.

"What?"

"I can't get up either."

Colin reached down and took one of her outstretched hands. She clasped her other hand around his wrist and squeezed it tight while she pulled herself up. Colin braced himself against his walking stick until she was upright, then she released him and resumed flailing her arms to the music.

"Come on Colin," she shouted.

Colin smiled and shook his head. He stepped back,

away from Louise's grasping hands. "No, that's enough for me. I need to sit down for a bit."

Colin limped to his armchair and slumped into it with a sigh. His arms and legs ached and he felt a bit light-headed from his exertions. He wondered if Tony Harris would let him have a go on his oxygen mask, but didn't have the energy to go and ask him. The Varukers' Thatcher's Fortress blasted out of the speakers and he watched Louise shuffle around to it. He shook his head and smiled. He rested his head against the back of his armchair and closed his eyes, wondering where she got all her energy from.

* * *

After dinner, while the workfare assistant cleared the dining table and wheeled it out of the way, Colin took Dave Turner and Louise Brown through the French doors into the back yard. They stood by the ten-foot high gate, looking at a pair of heavy bolts securing it at the top and bottom.

"What do you reckon?" Colin asked.

"The bottom one should be easy enough," Dave said, "but what about the top one?"

"Maybe I could reach it with my stick?"

Dave shook his head. "Nah mate, you'd never get it open with that."

Colin lifted his walking stick and stretched up onto his toes. His hand shook. The walking stick wavered wildly in the air, impossible for him to control. He gripped the walking stick in both hands but it made little difference to his coordination. Louise joined him from behind and held his wrists to steady them. Colin felt her hot breath on his neck, the spikes of her hair jabbing into the back of his head. Together they manoeuvred Colin's walking stick, inch by inch, closer to the bolt's sliding grasp.

"Hold it there," Dave said. He grabbed the centre of Colin's walking stick and yanked it toward him. The rubber end slipped off the bolt grasp and Dave stumbled backwards. "Bollocks," he said. "I told you it wouldn't fucking work."

"Yeah well, how else are we supposed to open it?" Colin asked. He lowered his walking stick and leaned on it, stared up at the bolt.

"I reckon we'd need something to stand on," Louise said. Colin turned to look at her. She smiled and shrugged. "Chair or something?"

"It'd need to be a fucking big chair," Dave said.

Louise frowned. "Yeah well, I'm only saying. You got any better ideas then?"

Dave shook his head.

"Maybe there's a ladder somewhere?" Colin said. "Otherwise how would they have locked it in the first place?"

Dave shrugged. "Well if there *is* a ladder, I've never seen it. That gate hasn't been opened in the ten years I've been living here."

"Yeah well," Colin said, "we're going to have to get it open somehow, or the whole fucking day's a write-off."

Colin heard a window slide open upstairs and the sound of trippy technobabble drifted out. He looked up, saw the retirement home manager lean out of the window and glare at him.

"Oi you lot. Get back inside."

"We're going to need to do something about that cunt too," Colin said quietly.

49

* * *

Biffo Ratbastard sat in the driver's seat of his electric transit van, waiting for the traffic light to change to green. Mike Hock sat in the passenger seat. He drummed his fingers on the roof of the van through the open window while he hummed a song to himself. Fungal Matters was in the back of the van with his drum kit. His dog, Gristle, lay by his side next to a box of merchandise left over from Sick Bastard's last tour in the late-2030s. By his feet was another box containing Biffo's Samson microphone, a small four-channel mixing board, and assorted cables and couplers.

The traffic light changed to red and amber. Biffo floored the accelerator and the van lurched forward with a loud hum. Fungal swore as he was catapulted back. Biffo drove up Shefferham High Street, past rows of pound shops and charity shops, boarded up shops that used to be newsagents or fruit and veg shops, following the directions given by Ozzy Osbourne's voice on the van's GPS device.

"Next fucking left, you cunt," the GPS said in a shaky Birmingham accent.

Biffo turned onto a side road and bumped up the kerb into a pedestrian area lined with trees. Two policemen in riot gear watched them pass. Biffo resisted the urge to give them the finger. The last thing he needed right now was hassle from the coppers.

"Next fucking right, you cunt."

Biffo turned right, into a residential area. Dilapidated terraced-houses passed by outside the van's window.

"Next fucking right, you cunt."

Biffo saw the place he was looking for half-way down the street, and pulled up outside it.

"You're fucking here, all right?" The GPS said. "Now

fuck off and leave me alone."

Biffo switched off the motor and climbed out of the van. He looked at a twenty-foot high, barbed-wire-topped wall. *Retirement Home SY-468*, a sign read on a solid metal gate built into the wall, *Your happy days end here.* Biffo smiled. He had no doubt that was a true statement, but with a completely different meaning to the one it was intended to convey. The place looked like a prison, and Biffo wouldn't be surprised if he saw gun turrets and guard dogs once they got through the gate. He pressed an intercom button by the side of the gate, held it in for a few seconds.

"Yeah?" a voice said through a speaker. "What do you want?

"We're here to pick up Steve Snitch."

"Who?" the voice asked.

"Steve Snitch."

"Never heard of him."

"He was in a band called Sick Bastard, they're playing a gig tonight? It's been arranged with your manager."

"Oh, him. Yeah, he's been driving us all daft with his noise all day. You can take him any time you want. Keep him for all I care."

The gate buzzed and swung open with a whir of electric motors. Biffo climbed into the van and drove though the gate. The gate closed behind him with another whir.

"Fucking hell, what a dump," Mike Hock said.

Biffo nodded. Retirement Home SY-468 was a drab-looking prefabricated building with white-washed walls turning yellow with age and neglect. Dirty windows gave no clue as to what lay inside. Biffo drove up to the front door and parked next to a gleaming red Porsche on the gravel drive. He climbed out and slammed the van door.

Mike opened the van's back door to let Fungal Matters and his dog out. Biffo walked up to the retirement home door and pushed against it. It was locked. He pressed a button on an intercom at the side of the door.

"Yeah?"

"We're here to pick up Steve Snitch?"

"Oh yeah, all right then."

The door buzzed and Biffo pushed through it into a reception area. It smelled of disinfectant, with a faint whiff of urine and boiled cabbage. A man sitting behind a desk looked up from an entoPAD.

"He'll be in the lounge, it's down there." The man pointed left down a corridor. "No dogs allowed in here," he said when Mike Hock and Fungal Matters walked through the door.

"It's a blind dog," Mike said.

"I don't care if it's deaf as well, you can't bring it in here. It's health and safety, no dogs allowed."

"But –"

"It's okay mate," Fungal said to Mike, "I'll wait outside.

Biffo and Mike walked down the corridor, following the sound of Steve Snitch's de-tuned electric guitar, until they came to a green door. Mike pushed it open and Biffo looked inside. The smell of urine and boiled cabbage was much stronger in the open-plan lounge than it had been in the reception. Old people dressed in stained nightwear sat in battered armchairs lined along the walls of the room. Some were asleep, oblivious to the wails and screeches coming from Steve Snitch's guitar, others stared down at entoPADs resting on their laps.

"What a fucking miserable place," Biffo said. Mike smiled and nodded.

An old man sitting close to the door caught Biffo's eye.

He had a fading red anarchy symbol tattooed on the side of his wrinkled bald head, just above the right ear. An old, jagged scar on his neck stood out in a deep purple from the grey, pallid tone of the surrounding skin. Before him stood a walking frame covered in stickers displaying the logos of lots of different punk bands from the 1980s to the mid-2020s. Biffo couldn't resist walking over to examine the walking frame in more detail to see if he could spot Sick Bastard's logo anywhere. He found one near the bottom of the front left leg, and pointed it out to Mike Hock.

The old man looked up from his entoPAD and stared at Biffo. His eyes went wide and his mouth gaped open. The entoPAD slipped from his fingers and dropped to the floor.

Biffo bent down and picked up the entoPAD, placed it back in the man's shaking hands. "Here you go mate," he said. The man stared at Biffo, but said nothing.

Biffo turned away and walked toward Steve Snitch, who was sitting in the far corner of the room. Steve wore the same black and red striped pyjamas he had been wearing for their rehearsal earlier in the week. His slippered feet were stretched out before him, resting on top of a small practice amp. Chrome-plated finger protector rings on his right hand slid up and down the fretboard, while metal finger picks on his left hand plucked the guitar's strings. He looked down at the guitar while he played, his tongue lolling out in concentration.

"Snitchy, you cunt," Biffo shouted.

Steve Snitch startled and stopped playing. He looked up at Biffo and grinned. "All right Ratty, you old fucker. Good to see you again. So how's life back in the outside world?"

"Fucking shite, same as always," Biffo said, smiling. He looked around for somewhere to sit, couldn't find anywhere. "So you ready to fucking rock then, or what?"

"Yeah," Steve said, "just need to get my dreads and I'm all set. Can't fucking wait to get back on stage."

Biffo nodded. "Yeah, you and me both. But change out of those pyjamas first, we're not a fucking Boomtown Rats tribute band."

Steve laughed. "Yeah, no worries. Give me ten minutes and I'll be all sorted."

Steve grunted as he sat forward and shuffled his feet off the practice amp. He leaned over and rested his guitar against the amp. Loud feedback whistled from the speaker. A man nearby clasped his hands over his ears. Another fiddled with his hearing aid.

Mike Hock walked over and switched the amp off, then unplugged Steve's guitar and swung its strap over his shoulder. "I'll take this out to the van and check up on Fungal," he said.

"All right, Cocky?" Steve said. "Ratty got you fetching and carrying then?"

Mike nodded. He smiled. "Yeah, he's still the same old fucking slave driver."

"Give us a hand getting up then, Cocky." Steve held out a hand and Mike clasped it, pulled him onto his feet. Steve grimaced. "Fucking hell, my legs are getting worse." He limped across the threadbare carpet with Mike and they left the lounge together.

Biffo eased himself into the armchair Steve had vacated and took out his electronic cigarette. He puffed on it, occasionally glancing at the door.

The old man with the anarchy tattoo struggled to his feet and hobbled across the room. His back was arched, almost bent double over the walking frame as he inched his way closer. Several minutes passed before he stood before Biffo. His wheezing breath came in short, gasping pants. His face had turned a bright red colour.

"You all right mate?" Biffo asked. He took another drag on his electronic cigarette while he waited for the man to catch his breath.

"Didn't you used to be Biffo Ratbastard?" the man finally asked, in a rasping, hoarse voice.

Biffo nodded. "Yeah, mate. Still am, in fact."

"I've got all Sick Bastard's records and CDs," the man said, proudly. "I've not got nothing to play them on, mind, but they were a fucking great band."

"Thanks. They're all on entoTUNES now, so you could listen to them on there if you wanted?"

"Yeah. Not the same though, is it? I couldn't believe it when they moved Steve Snitch in here. Does being in a band not make much money then? I thought you'd all be fucking loaded."

"Ah, we never did it for the money," Biffo said. "Not like them 1970s tossers. Besides, Old Snitchy had an expensive operation to pay for, that's how he ended up in here. He blew all his savings on it, couldn't support himself no more."

The old man shook his head. "Damn fucking shame that. Still, it's been good having him here. He plays his guitar to us every night and we all have a sing-song before bed time. So what are you doing here then, you moving in too?"

Biffo laughed. "Nah mate, they'll never get me in a place like this. I'm just here to pick Snitchy up. We're reforming Sick Bastard, we've got a gig tonight at one of the other –" Biffo almost said death homes, and managed to catch himself just in time. "–retirement homes."

The old man's eyes widened. "No fucking way. You need a roadie?"

"Not really," Biffo said. He watched the old man's face drop, his shoulders slump. "But you're welcome to come along with us if you want?"

"Yeah, that'd be fucking great. Can my bird come too?" He gestured with one hand at a frail-looking old woman sitting by the door.

Biffo shrugged. "Yeah, no worries. You'll need to go in the back of the van with the equipment though."

"Great, thanks, I'll go get her. You won't leave without us?" Biffo shook his head. The old man hobbled away. "Oi Brenda, guess what?" he shouted.

A few minutes later he returned with the old woman, Brenda, clinging onto his arm.

"Is that right what my Brian here says, you're taking us out for the night?" Brenda asked.

Biffo nodded. "Yeah, that's if you want to come. Do you like Sick Bastard too then?"

Brenda smiled. "Of course I fucking do. So when are we going then?"

"I'm just waiting for Snitchy to get dressed, then we'll be off. You'll be okay in the back of the van with the drums and shit?"

"Yeah. Don't worry, I'm not as fragile as I look. I used to live in a campervan before the bastards caught up with me and dragged me into this fucking dump." She sighed. "Still, I wouldn't have met my Brian here if they hadn't." She looked at Brian and smiled. Brian smiled back.

"Are we fucking off then or what?" Steve Snitch shouted from the doorway.

Biffo looked up and smiled. Thick, grey dreadlocks were gaffer-taped to either side of Steve's bald head, and hung down his shoulders like twines of crusty rope. He held a red baseball cap with a black Sick Bastard logo patch sewn onto it in his left hand. He wore camouflage shorts and huge black Doc Martens, and a red and black striped mohair jumper that was at least three sizes too big for him. He placed the baseball cap on his head, covering the gaffer-tape. The finished effect was striking, and took several years off him.

"Looking good there, Snitchy," Biffo called out. He stood up and gestured at Brian and Brenda. "Come on then, if you're coming. If you want to get dressed or something first we'll be waiting outside in the van."

"No, it's okay," Brian said, "we'll come as we are."

"You sure?" Biffo asked. "It's a bit cold out."

"Yeah, we'll be fine."

When he reached the doorway, Biffo turned to wait for the old couple to catch him up. Brian hobbled across the room painfully slowly, his walking frame inching across the carpet. Brenda sauntered by his side, keeping pace with him.

Back in the reception area, Biffo turned a latch on the main door and held the door open while Steve Snitch walked through. A shrill alarm sounded. The man sitting behind the desk jumped to his feet and rushed toward the door.

"Where do you think you're going?" he asked, shouting to be heard above the sound of the alarm. He grabbed Steve by the arm and pulled him back inside. The alarm silenced.

"Got a fucking gig to get to, haven't I?" Steve said. He tried to wrestle his arm free, but the man held him tight. "Fucking get off me, you cunt."

"Look mate," Biffo said to the man, "we've got permission to take him out for a few hours. Check with your manager if you don't believe me. We've already been through this twice already, you said we could take him."

The man looked at Biffo. "You'll need to sign him out first, and he'll need a GPS tag in case he gets lost. You understand that you're responsible for his safety the second he walks through that door? If anything happens to him it's nothing to do with us."

"Yeah," Biffo said. "It was all in the forms I had to sign."

The man wrestled Steve toward the desk. He took a thin yellow plastic strap from a desk drawer and fastened it around Steve's wrist. He picked up a hand-held scanner and scanned a bar-code printed on the yellow strap. The scanner beeped and the man released Steve's arm.

"It's too fucking tight," Steve said, pulling at the strap.

The man shrugged. "You'll get used to it. And don't even think about taking it off because I'll know about it if you do." He picked up his entoPAD and turned to Biffo. "I'll need your thumb-print to sign him out, then he's all yours." He held out the entoPAD and Biffo took it.

"These two are coming as well," Biffo said. He pointed a thumb at Brian and Brenda.

The man looked at the old couple and shook his head. "First I've heard of it. I was told there was just one going out tonight."

"Are you sure? I distinctly remember stating three people on the forms. Maybe you should go and check with your manager? I wouldn't want you to get into trouble by delaying us any further than you have already."

The man glared at Biffo. Biffo smiled back. The man shrugged. "Fair enough, take them all. But make sure they're back by nine-thirty, or I'll need to send someone to collect them."

"Not a problem," Biffo said, still smiling.

After Brian and Brenda had their GPS straps attached, Biffo pressed his thumb against the entoPAD and handed it back. Then they joined Mike Hock and Fungal Matters, who were waiting outside by the van.

* * *

Colin Baxter sat in his armchair. He held his entoPAD up in front of his face and peered over the top at the workfare assistant. It was coming up to the end of the assistant's shift for the day and he walked around the lounge, checking everyone was okay before handing over responsibility to his replacement. Fiona Scott was asleep, slumped over in her armchair and snoring loudly. The assistant prodded her awake and asked if she needed anything. Fiona stared up at him, but said nothing. The assistant grunted and moved on, Fiona went back to sleep. He reached Louise Brown and asked if she needed anything.

"Yeah, I need a piss," Louise said.

"Well go and have one, then."

Louise stood up and walked to the door. She looked over her shoulder and winked at Colin. Colin nodded and smiled back. The workfare assistant continued his end-of-shift rounds. By the time he reached Colin, Louise had returned. She raised a thumb to Colin and retook her seat.

"You need anything?" the assistant asked Colin.

"Nah mate, you're all right," Colin said.

The assistant turned to Dave. "You need anything?"

"Nope."

The workfare assistant moved on. When he finished his tour of the lounge he left the room. Colin looked at Dave and nodded. Louise was already on her feet and moving toward the lounge door. Colin and Dave joined her. Colin pulled a triangular block of wood he had found in the store-cupboard from his pocket. While Dave and Louise wrestled with Fiona Scott's armchair, Colin wedged the block of wood under the door and kicked it into place with his slipper. He joined Louise and Dave, and together they pushed Fiona's armchair against the door. Fiona didn't stir from her sleep.

"You think that will hold it?" Louise asked.

"Should do," Colin said. "Is The Gestapo secure upstairs?"

Louise smiled. "Yeah. I tied a belt round the handle to his office door, tied it to the door opposite. As long as nobody goes upstairs he'll be in there for the night."

Dave plugged his entoPAD into the lounge's speakers and The Exploited's Fuck The System blared out. Colin walked over to the French doors and opened them. He went back to the dining table and tried to push it toward the doors. The table's castors were stiff, unresponsive.

"Give us a hand with this," he shouted.

Dave helped him push the table through the French doors, while Louise picked up a foot-stool and followed them. They pushed the table out into the back yard and up against the gate. Louise put the foot-stool down in front of the table.

"So who's doing it then?" Colin asked. "I don't reckon I'll be able to, what with my bad knee and everything."

"I should be able to manage it," Dave said.

He put a hand on Colin's shoulder to steady himself while he climbed onto the foot-stool. He leaned forward and grabbed the top of the table, shuffled his stomach onto it. His legs kicked out wildly and his slippers flew off.

"Be careful," Louise said.

Dave brought his knees up under him and reached out for the gate while he pulled himself to his feet. He stretched up and gripped the bolt grasp. He tugged and twisted. The bolt moved millimetre by millimetre before springing free.

Dave grinned down. "Got the fucker." His smile faded. "Oh fuck, it's a long way down."

"Just come down the same way you went up," Louise said.

Dave crouched down, sliding his back down the wooden gate. He sat down on the table with his legs dangling over the edge. Colin and Louise took hold of a foot each while Dave shuffled onto his stomach.

"We've got you, mate," Colin said, "just jump off."

Dave shuffled himself backwards. Colin and Louise moved their grip up to his knees, ready to let him slide into their arms when he fell. Dave didn't move any further.

"You sure you've got me?" he asked.

"Yeah mate," Colin said.

Dave's fingers squeaked as they slid across the table. He dropped. Colin and Louise staggered back as they caught him between them.

"Well done," Louise said. She hugged Dave briefly, then picked up the foot-stool and took it back inside. Dave retrieved his slippers and shuffled his feet into them.

Colin clapped his hand on Dave's shoulder. "Yeah, well done mate. We'll just shift the table away from the gate and leave it out here, it's not as if we'll be needing it tonight."

When Colin and Dave returned to the lounge, Louise was swinging her arms around to The Exploited's Never Sell Out. Colin joined her, Dave sat down in his armchair.

* * *

Thumps and bangs could be heard on the lounge door during the two-second gap between songs. Nobody took any notice. Not even Fiona Scott, who must have been able to feel the vibrations through the back of her armchair. The whole lounge buzzed with geriatric excitement. Thatcher was back on her feet and being punched from all directions. I Still Fucking Hate Thatcher balloons sailed through the air, batted from one side of the room to the other. Everyone laughed, having a good time. Even Frank Sterner had given up complaining about the rowdy 80s and 90s music not being as good as music used to be in the 1970s, and joined in with the festivities.

Colin sat in his armchair, tapping his foot rapidly to the music. On his lap lay Greg Lomax's entoPAD, Louise having handed it to him earlier. He had the entoMAIL app open, and waited for a message. He smiled when it came. He turned to Dave Turner and shook him awake.

"Beer's here," Colin said when Dave looked at him.

Colin grabbed his walking stick and pushed himself upright. He slipped Greg's EntoPAD into his back pocket and looked down at Dave, who had remained seated.

"Well come on then, you lazy fucker. It's beer o'clock, what are you waiting for?"

Dave nodded and rubbed his eyes before rising. Colin opened the French doors and stepped out, walked up to the gate with Dave following close behind. Dave crouched down and slid the bottom bolt back. He straightened up and pulled open the gate. Rusted hinges screeched in complaint. Colin peered out at a young man with long, scraggly brown hair.

"Greg Lomax?" the man asked. Colin nodded. "Delivery for you."

The delivery man held out an entoPAD with its screen facing Colin. Colin glanced at the screen and prodded a button marked Accept Delivery. Greg's entoPAD chimed and Colin took it from his back pocket. He looked at the screen, it asked him to confirm a payment to Boozy Suzy, 16 Glencose Avenue, Shefferham. Colin confirmed the payment and the delivery driver's entoPAD chimed in response.

The delivery man looked at his screen and nodded. "Right then, I'll just get it unloaded from the van. Where do you want it?"

Colin pointed through the French doors, into the lounge. "Just in there, mate."

The delivery man opened the back of his van and climbed inside. He let down a metal ramp and wheeled out a trolley containing a shrink-wrapped pallet of thirty-six two-litre plastic bottles of Yorkshire Bitter. He slid the ramp back into the van, closed and locked the van door, and pushed the trolley through the gate.

"Oi, you with the hair, what's going on down there?" the retirement home manager shouted from the upstairs window. "Is that alcohol? There's no alcohol allowed on these premises, you'll need to take it back."

The delivery man looked up and shrugged. "Nothing to do with me, I just do what I'm told. You'll need to take it up with whoever ordered it."

"So who ordered it then? Because I can assure you it wasn't me, and nobody else has that kind of authority."

The delivery man smiled at Colin and winked. "No idea. Like I said, I just do what I'm told."

"Well I'm telling you to take it back."

"Yeah well, you just said you didn't place the order, so it's not your decision."

"Wait there, I'm coming down." The manager disappeared for a few seconds, then returned. "Why won't this door open? You there, Baxter, go and tell the assistant there's something wrong with my door."

"Yeah, in a minute," Colin said, "I'll just sort this guy out first, see if I can find out what's going on for you."

The delivery man pushed the trolley into the lounge and unloaded the pallet of beer. He took out a Stanley Knife and slashed at the plastic wrap, tore it off and dropped it on the trolley. "Right then," he said to Colin, "that's me done." He looked at the Happy Thatcher Day banner draped across the lounge wall, the black balloons flying through the air, the spasmodic jerks of the dancing residents. He smiled. "Have a good one, yeah?"

Colin nodded. "Thanks mate, you too. Happy Thatcher Day." He pointed at Thatcher lying on her back in the centre of the lounge. "If you want to give her a bit of a kicking before you go, feel free."

The delivery man smiled and rubbed his hands together. "Don't mind if I do." He walked over and kicked Thatcher in the ribs, sent her flying across the room. "That's for my granddad, you fucking bitch."

* * *

Biffo Ratbastard heard a crash of cymbals and a chorus of expletives from the back of the van when he drove over a speed bump.

"You lot all right back there?" he asked. He grinned at Mike Hock in the passenger seat.

"No we're fucking not," Fungal Matters said. "Fucking slow down, you cunt, this is valuable equipment and I don't want it fucking wrecked."

"Next fucking right, you cunt," the GPS said. Biffo swerved into a side-street, causing another round of tumbling drums and swearing from the back.

"Are we nearly there yet?" Brenda asked. "Only I'm desperate for a piss."

"Oh that's just fucking great," Fungal said, "now I'm going to get soaked in fucking piss. Remind me again why I'm doing this?"

"Same reason as the rest of us," Biffo said. "Because you fucking love it. Brings it all back, doesn't it? I remember in the old days, when we was on tour we'd be living in a van like this together for months on end. I doubt any of your bands were any different."

Fungal grunted. "Yeah well, when I was in Society's Rejects we had a fucking massive motorhome, not a shitty little transit van. Being signed to a big label had its fucking perks, you know."

"Yeah, and they bled you dry for it. At least we kept our independence, no fucker in a suit to suck all our money away and tell us what we couldn't put on our records."

"Too fucking right," Mike agreed, nodding. "Remember that song about what's-his-face, the politician who fucked all those little kids?"

"That were just the one song," Fungal said. "How were we supposed to know the cunt would be found innocent? Everyone knew he just fucking bribed his way out of it. Anyway, we put that song out as a bonus track on our Worst Of compilation ten years later, so it's not like they squashed it forever."

Biffo laughed. "Yeah, after the cunt died so there was no fucker to sue you."

"Next fucking right, you cunt," the GPS said.

"Aye up," Mike Hock said. He leaned forward and pointed through the windscreen. "I reckon that looks like the right place there."

It was another miserable-looking building surrounded by a high wall, just like the one Biffo had picked up Steve Snitch and the old couple from. The GPS confirmed it as Biffo pulled up at the main gate.

"You're fucking here, all right? Now fuck off and leave me alone."

"Well that's the right place, all right," Biffo said, looking out of the side window. "But the guy said we need to go round the back."

"Try a bit further down the road," Mike said, "maybe there's a back alley or something."

Biffo cruised down the road. The high wall surrounding the retirement home gave way to a row of boarded up terraced houses. From one of the houses a baby cried, and someone yelled at it to shut up. Outside another sat a bedraggled-looking young man who stared at Biffo through vacant eyes as the van drove by.

"There!" Mike shouted, pointing.

Biffo spun the steering wheel and the van lurched to one side. He braked at the opening to a narrow alleyway and reversed to line up the van before swinging into it. He drove slowly past the backs of the terraced houses, until he came to a high wall topped with barbed wire. He parked near a large wooden gate built into the wall and switched off the van's motor. He pulled the keys from the ignition and spun them around his finger before pocketing them. Mike opened the passenger door and climbed out.

Biffo took an entoPAD from the van's glove compartment and composed a message to Punk76, the organiser of the gig, to let him know they had arrived. He put the entoPAD back in the glove compartment without waiting for a reply. He got out and opened the back door. Steve Snitch stumbled out, complaining about his legs. Brenda followed him and walked further into the alley, out of sight behind the van. Biffo heard the sound of urine hitting pavement, accompanied by a long sigh from Brenda.

Fungal Matters eased himself out of the van with his arms outstretched. His dog trotted after him and took up a position by his left side. Fungal reached down and patted the dog, then picked up its reigns. Brian shuffled to the edge of the van and sat there while he waited for Brenda to return and help him down.

Biffo heard a bolt slide open on the other side of the gate and turned toward it. The gate creaked open a few inches and an old man with short white spikes on one side of his otherwise bald head peered out.

"Punk76?" Biffo asked.

The man nodded, and pulled open the gate. "Yeah, mate. The name's Colin though. Thanks for coming, we really appreciate it. Happy Thatcher Day."

Biffo smiled. "Happy Thatcher Day."

"It's just through here," Colin said, and turned away, "but don't take too long getting your stuff out of the van, we need to get this gate locked so nobody else can get in."

"You going to give us a hand?" Biffo asked, but the man had already gone. He sighed. "I guess not."

Another old man appeared at the gate. "All right, Biffo?" he said. He wore a thick pair of spectacles, which slid down his nose when he nodded his head at Biffo. He pushed them back into position with a bony index finger. "Old Colin there's a right lazy cunt, but I'll give you a hand with your stuff if you like. I'm Dave."

"Cheers, Dave," Biffo said, "I really appreciate it."

Mike Hock and Steve Snitch had their guitars slung over their shoulders and stood by the side of the van, watching while Fungal felt inside for parts of his scattered drum kit.

Brian and Brenda stood nearby. They both shivered in their thin night clothes.

"Watch out mate," Biffo said to Fungal, "I'll get your drums for you, you just make your way inside. The gate's just there." He pointed at the gate, then felt foolish for doing so.

"Cheers," Fungal said. "Be careful with my drums, though."

"Yeah, I will."

Biffo climbed into the back of the van and rounded up Fungal's drum kit. He held a pair of snare drums out to Dave. Dave took them and carried them through the gate cradled in his arms. Biffo climbed out of the van with a large bass drum held between both hands.

"I'll take this, you two grab some of them other bits and bobs and follow me inside," he said to Brian and Brenda.

Brian frowned and rattled his walking frame. "What, and balance them on this, you mean?"

Biffo looked at the walking frame and nodded. "Yeah, fair point. You wait here and make sure no fucker pinches anything then. How about you, darling, you okay to carry some shit for us?"

"Yeah, okay," Brenda said. She picked up a cymbal stand.

Biffo turned away and carried the bass drum through the gate.

"Who the fuck are you lot?" a voice called out from above.

Biffo looked up at a young man in his mid-thirties leaning out of an upstairs window. "Sick Bastard," he called out.

"You fucking what?"

"Sick Bastard."

"You cheeky old cunt, I'll have you for that."

Biffo laughed. "I'd like to see you fucking try."

Biffo walked through a set of French doors into a large, open-plan lounge. Anti Nowhere League's So What blared out of a pair of large speakers either side of the room. Biffo counted thirty people in the lounge, all sitting in armchairs, most tapping their feet and jerking their shoulders to the music. Black balloons lay everywhere. A woman with spiked up blue hair waved at Biffo before lifting a two-litre bottle of beer to her mouth. Biffo smiled and nodded to her.

Fungal and Dave were assembling the snare drums by the far wall, between the two speakers. Biffo carried the bass drum over and put it down next to Fungal's dog. He tapped Dave on the shoulder to get his attention.

"Who's that geezer upstairs?" Biffo shouted into Dave's hearing aid.

Dave shrugged. "Just some cunt. Ignore him." He pointed to a corner of the room. "There's some beer over there, help yourself."

Biffo smiled and nodded. "Cheers, don't mind if I do."

Mike Hock and Steve Snitch stood by a pallet of plastic beer bottles, talking to Colin, the gig's organiser. They had already downed half a bottle each. Steve took a swig from his bottle and held it out to Biffo.

"Fucking great beer this, Ratty. Here, get some down your neck."

Biffo wiped the bottle's top with his shirt and took a long drink. He sighed, then belched and handed the bottle back to Steve.

"You seen who's here?" Steve asked, grinning. He gestured across the room with the beer bottle.

Biffo followed his gaze. His eyes widened. "Fuck me, it's Thatcher."

"Yeah, she's mine," Colin said. "I got her for my fiftieth birthday, I've kept her ever since. Fucking great for Thatcher Day parties."

"You're not fucking kidding," Biffo said. "You mind if I have a play with her?"

Colin smiled. "Be my guest."

Biffo walked over to Thatcher. He picked her up and set her on her feet, then swung his arm back and smacked her in the face. Thatcher flew backwards and landed on her back a few feet away. Biffo strolled up to her and kicked her between the legs, sent her skidding across the carpet toward one of the armchairs. The occupant of the armchair, an old woman, raised her walking stick and brought it crashing down into Thatcher's face.

"Fucking smart," Biffo said when he returned to Colin. "How much are you wanting for her? I'll give you a good price."

Colin shook his head. "The lady's not for selling."

Brenda carried in some more equipment from the van and put it down next to the drum kit. She bent down and patted Fungal's dog. The dog wagged its tail.

"Oi Brenda, is that the last of the stuff?" Biffo shouted. Brenda looked around and shook her head. She said something, but Biffo couldn't hear her over the music. Biffo turned back to Steve and Mike. "You going to stand here all night or are you going to help me get the rest of the stuff from the van?"

Mike shrugged. "Yeah, go on then. Catch you later, Colin. Don't drink all that beer without us."

They left the lounge and returned to the van. The man in the upstairs window shouted down at them, but they ignored him. Brian sat on the edge of the van tapping his fingers on the top of his walking frame. He looked up as they approached, and nodded. He pushed himself upright and shuffled to one side. Biffo leaned into the van and slid out a box of cables. He handed it to Mike and told him to take it inside. He gave Steve a tom-tom and hi-hat stand, and took out a box of merchandise for himself. He placed it on the ground and slammed the van door.

"That's the last of it, mate," he said to Brian. "Cheers for looking after the van for us."

"No worries."

Biffo carried the merchandise into the lounge and placed it on top of an electronic games table. He walked over to the box of cables Mike had put down near the drum kit and took out his mixing board. He looked around for something to stand it on.

Brian inched his way through the French doors and peered in. Brenda took up a position by his side and looped her arm through his. Brian's face cracked into a wide grin.

"Colin, you cunt," he shouted. "It's been a fucking long time since I saw that ugly mug of yours."

* * *

Colin turned to the French doors when he heard someone shout his name. An old man in striped pyjamas grinned in at him from the doorway, bent over a walking frame covered in multi-coloured blobs. An old woman in a yellow nightie stood by his side. Colin took another sip of beer and put the bottle down. He hobbled closer for a better look, and peered at the man as he came into focus. The multi-coloured blobs on the walking frame turned into band logos. A flash of recognition registered when Colin took in the anarchy tattoo on the side of the man's bald head, but it was the jagged scar on his neck that clinched it. Colin smiled and shook his head. He reached out and clasped the man on the shoulder.

"Fuck me," Colin said. He grinned like a lunatic. "Is that you, Bri?"

Brian smiled back and nodded. Colin stared at Brian's face, taking in the ravages of time that had taken their toll since the last time they had seen each other, some forty years ago at a Punks Reunited gathering in a pub in Cleethorpes. Brian had moved away fifteen years prior to that night, in search of work, and despite promises to stay in touch their friendship had soon degenerated to the occasional letter and an annual exchange of Christmas cards.

"Good to see you, mate," Brian said.

"Fucking hell, yeah," Colin said. "So how you been then? Any regrets?"

"Fucking loads, mate, how about you?"

Colin laughed. "Yeah, same here. Not that I'd want to change anything, mind. Except maybe not go to that fucking picket at Orgreave. My leg's never been the same since that fucking copper twatted me one."

"Yeah?" Brian said. He glanced down at Colin's knee. "Did you get any compensation for it when the truth about Orgreave finally came out?"

"Nah mate," Colin said, shaking his head. "I did apply, same as everyone else the bastards attacked that day, but they wouldn't pay up. The fuckers said because there was no record of me being employed as a miner at the time I must have been one of those anarchist infiltrators and it was my own fault for getting in the way."

"Fucking cunts," Brian said. "You should've taken it to court."

"Yeah well, couldn't afford it, could I? So anyway, how the fuck did you get here, then?"

"I'm in the same retirement home as Steve Snitch. Couldn't fucking believe it when Biffo Ratbastard turned up, I thought I must be fucking dreaming or something. Anyway, it turned out I wasn't, so when Biffo said they were playing a gig here I hitched a ride over with them." Brian gestured at the old woman by his side. "This is my bird, Brenda, by the way. She came too."

Brenda smiled. "All right, Colin? Brian's told me all about what you and him used to get up to when you was young."

"Yeah," Colin said, smiling at Brian, "they were fucking good times. Well come on in then, grab a seat and I'll get you a beer. You look fucking knackered, mate." Colin turned and gestured for Dave Turner to come over. "This is my mate Bri from the olden days," he said when Dave joined them and asked what was up.

"All right," Dave said. "So you're the famous Bri then, yeah?"

"Dave," Colin said, "can you check with Biffo if they've finished getting all their stuff in yet, and if they have can you go and lock the gate up?"

Dave nodded. "Yeah, will do."

"Then shut these doors, it's fucking freezing out tonight."

Colin led Brian and Brenda into the lounge. Brenda nodded her head in time to a UK Subs song as she walked by Brian's side. Colin saw Steve Snitch had set up a merchandise stall on the games table, and headed toward it. Louise Brown was already there, and swayed from side to side as she stared down at the merchandise. In her hand she held an almost-empty bottle of beer. She turned and lifted the bottle to her mouth just as Colin arrived.

"Colin, Colin, my old fucking mate, my old mucker," Louise said. She swung an arm around Colin's waist and stumbled. Colin reached out for the games table to steady himself when she lurched against him. "They brung some stuff with them, Colin, look. Look at all the stuff they brung." She held up a hand and wiggled her fingers through a fingerless black studded glove with a blood-red Sick Bastard logo printed on the back. "Look what I got, aren't they fucking great?"

Colin nodded. "Yeah, they look good." He picked up a Sick Bastard thermal vest and showed it to Brian. "Fucking smart or what? Just the job for cold winters."

Colin took out his entoPAD and bought the vest, then stuffed it down the back of his trousers, with Sick Bastard's logo hanging down like a bum-flap. Brenda bought an Old Fuckers With Attitude red woollen hat and pulled it down over her ears. Brian eyed up a pair of Sick Bastard slippers and complained to Steve Snitch about how much he was asking for them. When Steve wouldn't budge on price, Brenda paid for the slippers with her own entoPAD, then knelt down to help Brian put them on. She tossed his standard-issue retirement home plain brown slippers under the table.

Over by the drum kit, Biffo Ratbastard threaded audio cables along the back wall. He fixed them in place with a roll of gaffer tape from which he tore off strips with his teeth. The cables led to a small mixing board resting on the arm of Fiona Scott's chair in front of the lounge door. Fiona was asleep, her head slumped to one side, oblivious to the thumps and bangs from the other side of the door. Fungal Matters sat behind his drum kit, and took a swig from a bottle of beer. His dog roamed the lounge, sniffing the legs of each resident in turn. Mike Hock stood by the pallet of beer with his bass guitar slung over his shoulder. He watched Biffo while he drank.

A Chaos UK song that had just started playing was silenced when Biffo pulled the speaker cable out of Dave's entoPAD. There was a loud electrical pop when he plugged it into a coupler attached to another cable that led to the mixing board.

Someone outside the lounge thumped on the door and shouted "Open this door, it's time for your medication."

Colin sighed. "I'd best go and talk to him before he calls the fucking coppers."

"You're not going to let him in, are you?" Louise asked. Her voice slurred, and she stared at him with her head cocked to one side.

"Am I fuck."

Biffo tapped his finger on the microphone's wire-mesh head. The sound echoed through the speakers as a dull, metallic thud. "Oi," he shouted into the microphone, "Snitchy and Cocky, get your arses over here."

"Hello?" Colin shouted through the lounge door. "Is someone there?"

"Well it's about time, I've been banging on this door for nearly an hour, why didn't you answer before?"

"Didn't hear you, we had the music on."

"Why won't this door open?"

"Are you new?"

"What's that got to do with anything?"

"Sometimes the door sticks a bit, I'll try it from this end." Colin reached behind Fiona Scott's armchair and rattled the door handle. "It won't seem to turn, it must be broken inside."

"Well what am I supposed to do then? It says on my job sheet you need to have your medication now, and I can't find the manager anywhere."

Steve Snitch's de-tuned guitar blasted out of the speakers, soon followed by Mike Hock's bass. Fungal Matters joined in on drums, all three seemingly playing a different song. Steve shouted "Oi, oi, oi, oi, oi," repeatedly into the microphone.

"Sorry, I can't hear you," Colin shouted through the door. "Someone's put the music back on."

Biffo Ratbastard walked over to Fiona Scott's armchair and twiddled sliders on the mixing board resting on one of the arms. He walked into the centre of the lounge and stood listening for a few seconds, then returned to the mixing board and made some more adjustments. Seemingly satisfied with the overall sound after another trip to the centre of the lounge, he walked up to the microphone and gently pushed Steve Snitch out of the way.

Steve and Mike Hock stopped playing, Fungal Matters continued thrashing his drums for a few more seconds, then stopped. Fungal felt around on the floor for a bottle of beer he had placed there, and took a long drink. Biffo fine-tuned the angle of the microphone and looked around the lounge with a sneer.

"Right then, you cunts, time to get out of those fucking armchairs. Let's fucking have it. State Pension. One two three four."

A blast of feedback howled from Steve's guitar and mutated into a two-chord riff. Mike's bass gave out a low, rumbling dum dum dum dum, the same note over and over again. Steve stood in a Ramones stance, his legs far apart, his dreadlocks flying in all directions as he nodded and shook his head to Fungal's fast drum beat. Mike stood still, concentrating on his playing as the bass-line got more intricate. Biffo gripped the microphone stand in both hands and shouted the opening lyrics.

Colin felt a cold shiver down his spine, the music flowing through him and reminding him of good times. His shoulders twitched, his left hand thumped against the side of his leg. He leaned on his walking stick and tapped his foot, shouted along with Biffo at the chorus.

"State pension, state pension, state pension, give us back our, state pension, state pension, state pension."

Louise twirled around slowly, her arms swinging. She shuffled out of her mohair cardigan and tossed it to one side. Brian inched his way across the lounge toward the band, his head bobbing, a wide grin on his face. Brenda walked by his side, keeping pace with him.

"Come on, you fuckers, you're not dead yet," Biffo shouted, "get up and fucking dance."

Colin hobbled closer to the band. Brian stood a few feet away from Louise, just out of reach of her flailing arms. Brian pushed down on the top of his walking frame and stretched himself up onto his toes, then dropped down again, repeatedly bobbing up and down in an old man's pogo. Brenda punched the air by his side.

A few other residents took their lead and climbed out of their armchairs. Sharon Baker stood up and bent over. She clasped her hands together and swung her shoulders, twitched her feet. Greg Lomax remained seated. His head nodded, his right hand thumped down on the arm of his chair in time to the music. Fiona Scott woke up mid-way through the song and rubbed her eyes. She looked around, gaped at the band, and pushed herself onto her feet to join the dancers.

Colin brushed shoulders with Brian, being careful not to unbalance him. Brian raised a shaking hand from his walking frame and prodded Colin in the chest with a bony finger. Everyone was smiling, even Frank Sterner, who usually clapped his hands over his ears every time he heard music recorded after 1979. The retirement home's lounge buzzed with excitement the likes of which Colin hadn't seen in all the time he had lived there.

The song ended with a screech from Steve Snitch's guitar and a scream from Biffo Ratbastard. Everyone paused, took a panting breath while they rested. Biffo picked up a bottle and took a quick drink. He glared at the people still sitting in their armchairs.

"This is from our last album, Old Fuckers With Attitude," Biffo said. "It's called Not Dead Yet, and all you cunts who are still sitting down need to remember that. Come on, you lazy bastards, one two three four."

* * *

Biffo Ratbastard glanced behind him at Fungal Matters while the band played a short instrumental between verses. The poor old sod's face had turned purple keeping up with the machine-gun beat of the song, and Biffo feared for the man's heart. Sick Bastard's last drummer, Peter Vile, had suffered his first heart attack during a practice session, and it was only the quick intervention of Mike Hock that had kept him alive long enough for the ambulance to arrive. Biffo hoped history wasn't about to repeat itself. He turned back to the microphone in time for the next verse.

"You're all living in a fucking dream state," Biffo shouted, "you need to fucking wake up before it's too late. Beat the politicians at their own game, kill the bastards, it's time to take aim. Pick a side, but make sure it's the right one. That's the only way this war will be won."

Dozens of wrinkled, bony fists punched the air before him. The woman with the spiked up blue hair flailed her arms wildly and sang along with every word. Biffo ripped the microphone from its stand and clutched it in both hands. He bent over and screamed the chorus.

"War on poverty, war on hope. They take away our money so we just can't cope. War on terror, just an excuse. War on poverty, it's time to fucking choose."

Steve Snitch and Mike Hock stopped playing and the drum beat slowed. Biffo's repeat of the chorus slowed to a chant. Steve and Mike clapped their hands over their heads. Everyone in the audience, even those who still remained seated, clapped and chanted along.

"War on poverty. War on hope. They take away our money. So we just can't cope. War on terror. Just an excuse. War on poverty. It's time to fucking choose."

"Thanks," Biffo said to a smattering of applause. "Fucking true that, too," he added. He turned to check on Fungal. The drummer lay slumped over his bass drum, his naked back slick with sweat. Biffo propped the microphone back on its stand and rushed over. He grabbed Fungal's shoulder and shook him.

"What?" Fungal asked.

"Fucking hell mate, I thought you was dead for a minute there."

"Nah, just fucking knackered."

"You okay to carry on, or do you want to call it a night?"

"Give me a few minutes to get my breath back and I'll carry on."

"Good man," Biffo said. He patted Fungal on the back. "You're doing a fucking great job."

Biffo turned back to the audience. They were getting restless at the long delay between songs, mumbling to each other. Someone shouted "Get on with it, you cunts." Steve Snitch plucked out the opening notes to Ding Dong the Fucking Bitch is Dead and was met with a roar of approval. Biffo walked up to the microphone. He held out his hands, palms facing the audience. He smiled and nodded.

"All right, all right, we'll do the fucking Thatcher song." The audience cheered. "But it'll need to be the fucking acoustic version while Fungal takes a rest. Feel free to join in if you know the words, yeah?"

They knew the words, all right. Every wrinkled face in the audience sang along, their angry shouts almost drowning out Steve's wailing guitar. Fists were raised and punched the air, slippered feet pounded against the carpet. Loose floorboards bounced. Thatcher crowd-surfed toward Biffo, helped on her way with fists that tumbled her over and over. When she came close enough Biffo grabbed her and shook her. He closed his arm around her neck and held her in a headlock while he sang.

"Ding dong, you're fucking dead, we're all happy cause now you're dead, ding dong you're fucking dead at last. You've gone straight to fucking hell, so get down there and fucking yell, get down there and give the devil head."

Phlegm flew through the air and splattered into Thatcher's face. A sticky brown glob dripped from a blood-shot eye and crawled down her pointy nose like a squashed slug. Biffo caught a few splashes himself, but he didn't care. This was what he had been missing all those years since the band split up. That unique surge of adrenalin you only ever get when you're in front of an appreciative audience.

Biffo lifted Thatcher above his head and hurled her away from him. Fists rose up to meet her, batted her in all directions. Someone grabbed her leg and pulled her to the ground. Everyone surged around her, kicked out with slippered feet, bashed her in the face with walking sticks, stamped on her body with the legs of walking frames.

Biffo couldn't resist joining them. He pushed his way through the crowd around Thatcher and kicked out at her. Steve Snitch took up the vocal duties in his absence, but screams of "Fucking bitch," "You fucking evil cunt," "Die you fucking bitch," and similar war cries from everyone around Thatcher drowned him out.

Thatcher writhed and squirmed beneath their blows.

She lurched up when she was stamped on. A kick to the face sent her back down. Someone raised a walking stick and jabbed down on her neck. Thatcher hissed like an angry lizard and turned her head to one side. Her outstretched arms drooped, her body became flaccid. Slippered feet dug into her with a whump, making her judder and shake as she shrivelled away.

Biffo squeezed his way out of the crowd and returned to the microphone. Fungal Matters seemed to have recovered, his face no longer the colour of beetroot. Biffo nodded to him, then realised it was a pointless thing to do. Biffo picked up a beer bottle and took a long drink. He poured beer onto the palm of his hand and rubbed it over his head and face, then lifted his shirt and wiped it off. He looked out at the audience. They were still huddled around Thatcher, kicking and stamping on her.

"Money-Grabbing Bastard Politicians," Biffo shouted into the microphone.

Fungal took up the drum beat, a slow, thump thump thump on the bass drum, gradually speeding up when Mike's bass guitar joined in, and turning into an all-out thrash from the first discordant wail from Steve's lead guitar.

Thatcher was forgotten, stamped flat beneath the audience's angry feet. They turned back to Biffo, their anger now directed at all those who had taken Thatcher's place in the halls of power. Their greed, corruption and self serving that continued Thatcher's legacy right up to the present day, pushing ordinary working class people further and further into poverty while the politicians lined their own pockets and secured their own gold-plated future.

Biffo screamed the words and beat his fists by his sides. Steve Snitch stood close by, thrashing his head from side to side as his fingers slid up and down the guitar's fretboard. Steve's flying dreadlocks slapped against Biffo's face like rancid whips. Mike Hock circled around and took up a place to Biffo's right. Both he and Steve leaned into the microphone together and shouted the chorus along with Biffo. Steve struck up a Pete Townshend pose as the song drew to a close. He raised a hand high in the air and brought it swinging down to thrash against the guitar strings.

"Thanks," Biffo said to the cheers that greeted the song's end. "We're going to have to slow it down a bit now, we're not as young as we used to be, and you fuckers look like you could do with a rest too."

"Oi Biffo," the woman with the spiked up blue hair shouted, "remember these?"

She lifted up the front of her Vice Squad T-shirt, exposing flat, deflated breasts with a pair of Exploited skulls tattooed onto them. There was one on each breast, with the woman's nipples poking through the eye-sockets of each skull. She pulled the shirt over her head and lifted her arms, spun the shirt around in one hand.

Biffo smiled and nodded, though he had no idea who the woman was. He had a vague recollection of tattoos like those bouncing in his face somewhere in the midst of time, but couldn't remember where or when it was.

"Well I've got the Vaseline if you've got the Viagra," the woman shouted, and tossed the T-shirt at Biffo.

Biffo caught the shirt and wiped his face with it. The woman took a nipple between thumb and forefinger of each hand and stretched out her breasts, lifted them from her chest. She flapped them up and down, like rubbery wings.

Biffo tossed the Vice Squad T-shirt to one side. "Suits and Ties Tell You Lies," he shouted. The woman with the blue spikes whooped and raised her hands over her head. Her breasts dropped like a pair of lead-weighted balloons when she released them, and they flopped down against her chest with a slap. "One, two, three, four," Biffo shouted.

* * *

Colin couldn't tear his eyes away from Louise's breasts as they swung from side to side with the flailing of her arms. He knew from her stories that she was wild in her youth, but he never expected her to do anything like that. Not for the first time, he wished he could have known her when they were both young. Back when punk meant more than just an advertising slogan for corporations selling products to the elderly. She would have eaten him alive, he knew that, but it would have been worth it just to absorb a little bit of her energy and general don't-give-a-fuck attitude to life.

Colin inched his way toward her, leaning on his walking stick for support. Like most of the retirement home's residents, Colin's energy was flagging, and all he wanted to do was slump into his armchair and sit back to watch the rest of the show. Several residents had already done so, and sat exhausted but happy in their usual armchairs. Only a few remained standing, most of those content to stand still and watch the band. Brian and Brenda stood by the French doors, cooling down from a breeze blowing through them. Dave Turner stood to Louise's right, getting a good eyeful for himself. His arms swung by his sides, but there was little energy left in them.

Louise waved her hand in front of Colin's face. Colin looked up from her breasts. She poked her tongue out at him and smiled. "I'm up here," she shouted, and grabbed Colin's shoulders. She used them to propel herself up onto her toes, thumped back down onto the heels of her slippers, then pushed herself up again. Colin watched her breasts flap up and down.

"That was the last one," Biffo Ratbastard said when the song ended. Louise shouted for more, but Biffo shook his head. "We're fucking knackered, darling. You'll have to listen to us on entoTUNES instead."

Steve Snitch lifted his guitar strap over his head and propped the guitar up against Fungal's bass drum. He took Fungal by the arm and led him over to where the rest of the beer stood. He handed Fungal a bottle and took one for himself. Mike Hock joined them while Biffo unplugged all the cables.

Louise sighed and headed for her armchair. She sat with her hands clasped behind her head, her flat, tattooed breasts glistening with sweat.

"Open this fucking door, right now," the retirement home manager shouted, banging on the lounge door.

Colin looked at the door. He looked at Dave, who shrugged. Colin knew they would need to open the door sooner or later, and that there would be repercussions when they did, but he would rather it was later. Once they let the manager in that would be the end of the party, and Colin didn't want that just yet. He turned to Biffo and caught his attention.

"Fucking great gig, mate. Best fucking Thatcher Day ever. Well except for the first one, anyway, nothing could ever beat that."

"Thanks," Biffo said. "It's good to be playing live again, I've missed it. Shame about Thatcher."

Colin glanced at Thatcher, who lay discarded in the centre of the lounge. She stared back at him, her arms and legs strewn around her at odd angles, her body twisted. "Don't worry about it, that happens to her every year. A bit of glue and a patch and she'll soon mend. Are you staying for tea then? We're going to order some pizzas."

Biffo nodded at the lounge door, where the manager was still banging and shouting. "What about him?"

"Fuck him, he can wait."

"I wouldn't mind a pizza," Biffo said. He scratched the side of his face. "I'm fucking starving, I haven't had nothing since this morning and that beer's gone straight to my head. Talking of which, is there any of it left?"

Colin looked over at the stash of beer, where Steve, Mike and Fungal stood, drinking from a bottle each. "Yeah, I reckon there should be a few bottles left. You'll need to be quick though, the way them three are going through it."

Biffo laughed. "Yeah, nothing unusual there."

"Oi Colin," Brian shouted from the French doors. Colin turned to face him. Brian pointed into the back yard.

"What's up?" Colin asked.

"There's loads of fucking coppers in the alley outside, they say if we don't open the gate they're going to smash it down."

Colin and Biffo both walked to the French doors and looked out into the yard. They heard a whine of electronic feedback, then an amplified voice called out. "This is your last warning, if you do not open this gate we will have no choice but to open it by force."

"What should we do?" Brian asked.

Colin sighed. "The fucking Gestapo must've called them, we'd best open the lounge door and let him in. He can deal with the coppers, I'm not having anything to do with the cunts."

A loud thud against the gate made it judder in its frame. Brenda grabbed Brian's arm and told him he should move out of the way before the police got in, otherwise there was no telling what might happen to him. Colin agreed with her, and took Brian's other arm. Together, they both rushed him inside.

Dave Turner was already heading to the lounge door. Colin helped him push Fiona Scott's armchair out of the way. Fiona looked up from her entoPAD and giggled. Colin put his back against the door to hold it closed while Dave bent down and wiggled the block of wood out from underneath it.

There was a crash of splintering wood outside, and a lot of shouting. Six policemen wearing black body-armour and full-face helmets swarmed into the lounge waving tasers. Colin waited until Dave was clear of the lounge door, then stepped to one side. The door flew open and the retirement home manager ran in, a workfare assistant Colin had never seen before close behind him.

One of the policemen pointed his taser at the manager and pulled the trigger. Twin barbs flew out and embedded themselves in the side of the manager's face. He squealed like a pre-pubescent child and dropped, twitching, to the carpet.

"Taser, taser, taser," the policeman shouted. His voice echoed inside his helmet.

The workfare assistant skidded to a halt and raised his hands in the air. Another policeman tasered him. He screamed, and fell down next to the manager.

"Taser," the policeman said. He glared through his visor at the workfare assistant writhing on the carpet.

The other four policemen waved their tasers in all directions, as if not sure who they should be aiming at.

"Um..." Dave began. All the tasers spun to point at him. He raised his hands. "... is there something wrong?"

"What's been going on here?" one of the policemen

demanded. "We had a call there was some sort of disturbance in progress."

Dave shook his head, his hands still in the air. "Um ... Nothing. Just a little party for us old folks, that's all. A bit of music, a bit of dancing, that sort of thing."

The policeman grunted. "So who were those men who attacked us?" He pointed at the manager and workfare assistant.

"Those are our carers," Colin said, "they work here."

The policeman jerked his taser across to point at Colin's chest. Colin backed away, one hand raised, the other gripping his walking stick tightly.

"You with the blue hair," another policeman said, looking at Louise, "why are you undressed?"

"Because it's fucking hot," Louise said.

The policeman frowned, then grunted. He pointed at the manager and workfare assistant again. "And these two definitely work here?"

Louise nodded. "Yeah."

The policemen all looked at each other. One shrugged. Another swore. Two of them bent down and ripped the taser barbs from the manager and workfare assistant. Both men screamed and clutched their faces.

"Right, well," one of the policemen said, "just keep the noise down in future." They all turned to leave.

"Wait," Colin said. He pointed at the two men lying on the carpet. "Will they be okay?"

The policeman shrugged as he walked away. "Probably. They shouldn't have attacked us like that, so it's their own fault either way." He turned back to Colin and tapped a small camera mounted on his shoulder. "The evidence is all in here, should they wish to make a complaint about it."

Colin hobbled over to the retirement home manager and prodded him with his walking stick. The manager cried out and curled himself up into a trembling ball. Blood seeped through his fingers as he clutched his face.

"Pizzirrs on irrs way," Greg Lomax said.

Colin frowned down at the manager and workfare assistant. "I reckon we should probably call an ambulance while we wait."

* * *

They were all sitting in their armchairs eating pizza and listening to Never Mind The Bollocks piped through the retirement home speakers when the paramedics arrived. Biffo and the rest of Sick Bastard sat around the games table, two pizza boxes between them and a two-litre bottle of beer each. Brian sat in Frank Sterner's armchair, while Brenda perched herself on the arm next to him. Frank wandered the room, having already eaten his fill.

The paramedics were both dressed in green body-armour, and wore face-protecting helmets similar to the ones the police wore, except their helmets were white rather than black, and had a green cross printed on the front of them, just above the visor. They carried a stretcher between them, and one had a large bag slung over his shoulder. They put the stretcher down next to the workfare assistant and the one with the bag bent over him.

"Who's in charge here?" The other paramedic asked.

When nobody replied, Colin raised a hand. "It was me that called you, will that do?"

The paramedic looked at Colin. "Can you tell me their names?"

Colin wrestled to dredge the manager's name up from memory, but he had only ever heard him referred to as The Gestapo. If anyone had ever used his real name Colin hadn't heard it.

"Um ... no, sorry," Colin said. He pointed at the workfare assistant. "That one's new, he only started work here today. The other's the big boss, but I don't know his name."

"And they were both tasered, you say?"

"Yeah."

The paramedic nodded. He stepped over the workfare assistant and, together with the other paramedic, grabbed hold of the manager and hefted him onto the stretcher. They carried him out, then returned a few minutes later for the workfare assistant.

"Will they be okay?" Colin asked as they carried the stretcher across the lounge.

"Yeah, we get these all the time. They'll be right as rain in the morning. You lot got someone to look after you until then?"

"Yeah, we're fine," Colin said, "don't worry about us."

Colin returned to his pizza and pulled another slice from the box he shared with Dave Turner. He bit into it while he watched Frank Sterner shuffle by.

"So what are we doing after this?" Dave asked. He reached across for a slice of pizza.

Colin shrugged. "Dunno. I'm pretty fucking knackered, I reckon I might just veg out here for the rest of the night."

"There's still plenty of life left in me."

"Yeah, I noticed. You're not the only one, either." Colin nodded at Fiona Scott, who was bobbing her head to the music. "I've seen it in the others too. They're all a lot more alert than they usually are. And I've been thinking." He looked at his entoPAD, noting the time displayed in the corner of the screen. "It's been over a day since our last medication."

"Yeah, so?"

"Well think about it. What if there's something in it that makes us tired all the time?"

"Like what?" Dave asked.

Colin shrugged. "Dunno. Could be all sorts of stuff. All I know is I haven't been taking mine for a few days now, and I haven't been tired anywhere near as much as I used to be."

"I thought you said you was knackered."

"Well yeah, I am now. But that's just tonight, and there's a good reason for that. I mean in general. I think Louise has been doing the same as me, and that's why she's always got so much energy."

"I don't know," Dave said, shaking his head, "why would The Gestapo want us to be tired all the time? It wouldn't make sense."

"Yeah, I guess. It's just a theory."

"Besides," Dave said, "the drugs come from the local chemist and they wouldn't give us stuff we don't need."

"Did you take any drugs before you came to live here?"

Dave smiled. "Only for fun."

"Any illness you've developed since you moved in?"

"No."

"Me neither," Colin said. "And I only started feeling tired when I moved in here. And when I stopped taking the stuff they give us I stopped being tired."

Dave frowned. "Yeah, that is pretty fucking weird."

"I reckon we should see what everyone's like tomorrow morning, then get together and discuss it properly before

The Gestapo gets back. There'll be some who need it, old Greg for instance, and maybe Tony, but I reckon most of us don't."

* * *

Biffo Ratbastard took another slice of pizza from the box and took a large bite. He washed it down with a gulp of beer and wiped tomato sauce from his mouth.

"Fucking good scran, this," he said. He flapped the remains of the pizza slice up and down in his hand and belched. "I reckon I could get used to this."

"It's not fair, we don't get nothing like this in that dump they put me in," Steve Snitch said. "All we ever get is boiled fucking cabbage and soup, day in, day out. I fucking hate cabbage, me. It's fucking vile stuff."

"Aw, diddums," Mike Hock said, smiling.

"Fuck off, Cocky. Then there's the security, that does my fucking head in too. They won't let anyone out without one of these fucking things." Steve held up his wrist, showing the yellow GPS strap he wore. "And if you're not back on time a fucking alarm goes off and they come to fetch you."

"What is it?" Fungal Matters asked.

Steve looked at him. "Sorry mate, I forgot you can't see. It's a fucking GPS device, so they can track where I am all the time."

Fungal shook his head. "Fucking hell. I'm glad I don't have to put up with any of that sort of bollocks. The only way I'm leaving my house is in a fucking wooden box."

Biffo nodded. "Yeah, me too." He took another long drink of beer. "I don't care what fucking bollocks the government come out with about how much better it would be for me in one of their Death Homes, I'm staying put."

Steve frowned. "I wish I had the fucking choice."

"So anyway," Biffo said, "fucking great gig, yeah?" Steve and Mike nodded. Fungal, his mouth full of pizza, raised a thumb. "I reckon we should do a few more, maybe a mini-tour of all the local Death Homes. What do you think?"

"Sounds good to me," Steve said. "Especially if we get free beer and pizza."

"Fuck, yeah, that'd be great," Mike said.

Biffo smiled. "I'll get onto it first thing in the morning, see what I can organise. I reckon some of them might pay proper money instead though. Then we could use it to book a bit of studio time, put out a new album on entoTUNES."

* * *

Colin leaned over Brian's walking frame and hugged him goodbye. Brian patted him on the back with one hand and promised he would keep in touch now that he knew what Colin's entoPAD screen-name was.

"It's not really the same though, is it?" Colin said.

"No, mate. That's why I'm going to put in a transfer to move in here as soon as I get back."

"Me too," Brenda said.

They were standing in the back yard, near the smashed gate. The band's equipment had been carried out to the van and Biffo was sounding the horn, impatient to leave. Some of the residents had drifted off to bed, others sat in their armchairs finishing off the rest of the beer before they retired for the night.

"We'd best get going now, mate," Brian said.

Colin released Brian and he turned away, inched his way through the wreckage of the gate with Brenda at his arm. Colin stood at the gate and watched Brenda help Brian climb into the back of the van. She closed the door behind her.

"See you, Bri," Colin shouted.

"Yeah, see you, mate," came Brian's muffled reply from inside the van.

Biffo sat in the driver's seat, his elbow resting on the open window. "Fucking great night, thanks for booking us," he said, looking at Colin.

Colin nodded. "Yeah. Shame it has to end, really."

"We're putting on a local tour, so if you want us to come back again just send me a message and I'll sort it for you."

Colin smiled. "Yeah, that'd be fucking great. Whenever you like, we'll still be here."

Biffo nodded. "See you soon, then. Take care."

Colin waved as the van drove away. He sighed, then returned to the lounge and took up his regular seat. He picked up his entoPAD and smiled. Things were going to be different, he could feel it. The Gestapo, when he returned from hospital in the morning, wasn't going to have such an easy ride from now on.

The Snatcher (Remix)

At twelve years of age, Scar Gill knew he was too old for stories. He had responsibilities now that his father was dead. He guarded the village of Gold Thor's sheep from the scabbed ones who roamed the countryside, just as his father had done before him. It was an important job, and one that Scar Gill was proud to have. Gone were the carefree days of childhood. He was a man now, and soon it would be time for him to choose a wife and begin the task of creating a new generation.

But despite his age, Scar Gill still liked to hear the stories the village elder told in the evenings. Stories of the great Yarksher warrior of legend with the same name as him. Of The Snatcher, the Scar Gill of legend's arch nemesis, and the many battles they fought.

He knew they were only fanciful stories, that they couldn't possibly be true, but Scar Gill liked to imagine they were a real part of his family's history. That the Scar Gill of legend was a distant ancestor of his, and the warrior blood flowed through his body.

When the village elder called out to the children, Scar Gill crept closer to listen. He kept an eye on his sheep as he settled down behind an old oak tree, close enough to hear the stories, but far enough away not to be seen in the gathering dusk.

"Gather round, children," the elder said, "sit closer to the fire so The Snatcher's scabbed ones won't get you."

Scar Gill heard gasps from the younger children. He shivered involuntarily when he heard the name of the evil one, though he would never admit it to anyone. The Snatcher wasn't real, he told himself. She was just a monster invented to frighten children. Nobody would ever be so evil, it was impossible.

"Long, long ago," the elder began, "long before The Great Gee Had laid waste to our country, there was a village called That Lunn Don. It wasn't a small village like our very own Gold Thor, not even one like the mighty Barn Slay of which we were once a part. That Lunn Don was a vast metropolis, populated with many hundreds of people. Within its walls lived an evil witch, known as The Snatcher, who liked nothing more than to steal the milk from newborn infants.

"One day, The Snatcher decided this wasn't evil enough for her, and set in place her plan to rule the country so that she may steal much more than a baby's milk. So The Snatcher tricked the people of That Lunn Don into making her their queen. She promised them riches beyond imagination, said they would own their own dwellings and places of work if only they would make her their queen. But the people of That Lunn Don did not know her true intentions, for The Snatcher was wise and cunning as well as wicked and evil. On the very day she was crowned queen, The Snatcher set her dastardly plan into motion.

"She passed new laws to set the money lenders free from their chains. She created an army of Lords of the Land who were free to charge the people of That Lunn Don rents far in excess of what they could afford, making them reliant on charity to survive. Many travelling minstrels of the time sang songs of protest, but these fell on deaf ears and The Snatcher ruled for many years with an iron fist.

"It was not long before The Snatcher turned her steel gaze to the land of Yarksher and the riches it contained. The Under-dwellers, who had been supplying the village of That Lunn Don with their magical black rocks for many years, were the first of her targets. This angered The Under-dwellers, and they sent forth their champion, Scar Gill, to do battle with The Snatcher. Scar Gill was a mighty warrior, with many scalps to his name, but he was also a man of great compassion. He attempted to reason with The Snatcher, but his words fell on deaf, uncaring ears."

Scar Gill felt an immense pride well up within him as he listened from behind the oak tree. He imagined his warrior ancestor dressed in battle armour, standing bravely before the evil Snatcher. How The Snatcher would have trembled before him if it were not for her guards and their impenetrable ring of steel around her. How he, if he were the real Scar Gill of legend, would have fought through the guards and chopped The Snatcher's head off, put an end to her years of torment forever. He sighed. The sad part of the story was coming up.

"In retaliation for Scar Gill's effrontery," the elder continued, "The Snatcher decreed that she would seal up the caves from which The Under-dwellers extracted their magical black rocks. Without the black rocks to trade for food, The Under-dwellers were left hungry and destitute. Some of The Under-dwellers were so destitute they developed scabs upon their bodies, and The Snatcher took advantage of this. She used her evil powers to control the scabbed ones, to turn them against their fellow Under-dwellers."

Scar Gill wanted to shout "Boooooo," along with the children. But he knew he was too old for such things. He contented himself with striking his fist into his palm, cursing the scabbed ones for their traitorous ways.

"But Scar Gill held strong. His loyal Under-dwellers fought ferocious battles with the scabbed ones, and cast them from the villages of Yarksher for all time."

Scar Gill nodded to himself. Even to this day, the scabbed ones were still banished from Yarksher, and lived their cursed lives in the wastelands to the south of Barn

Slay, in the ruins of Notty Ham. Sometimes they would try to sneak back into Yarksher under cover of darkness and steal sheep, but they were always driven away because they were such a cowardly race.

The first time Scar Gill had seen a scabbed one he was just a small child. His father, Gold Thor's sheep watcher at the time, had caught a scabbed one on the fringes of the village one night, and paraded him through the village, bound in rope, the following morning. Scar Gill watched as the scabbed one was stoned to death by the whole village. He felt no pity. The scabbed ones deserved much worse than death for their betrayal in the times of The Snatcher.

"The Snatcher was not happy with the defeat of the scabbed ones," the elder continued. "She sent forth her Army of Blue Men from the village of That Lunn Don to lay siege against The Under-dwellers of Yarksher and their families. There was a great battle at the village of Org Reeve that took many lives on both sides of the conflict. But the Army of Blue Men had far superior weaponry to the sticks and stones of The Under-dwellers, and The Under-dwellers were defeated with mighty clubs and giant beasts.

"The caves of The Under-dwellers were sealed for all time. Entire villages who relied on trade from The Under-dwellers shrivelled and died. The Snatcher cackled in her castle while The Under-dwellers were forced to beg for scraps of food. All the riches of Yarksher were transferred to the village of That Lunn Don, while the people of Yarksher went hungry.

"But still The Snatcher was not satisfied. She created a new tax, one which everyone in Yarksher was forced to pay even if they were destitute and could not afford to do so. She used her Army of Blue Men to enforce the tax, throwing people into dungeons for the rest of their lives if they refused to pay.

"Scar Gill was angered by this. Although forced to live on the surface, The Under-dwellers had remained strong and formed communities together, so Scar Gill did not find it difficult to rally his army. They marched on the village of That Lunn Don, where they were joined by other armies. Armies from outside Yarksher. Armies from a land far away, where men wore skirts and spoke in a strange tongue."

A child giggled, and was hushed by the elder. Scar Gill smiled. He knew why the child had laughed. While the wives of The Under-dwellers themselves were fierce and strong, and fought alongside their men in the battles with The Snatcher's Army of Blue Men, the idea of men wearing skirts was preposterous. Somewhere down the ages, as the story was passed from generation to generation, this absurdity had entered the legend. Scar Gill vowed that if he lived long enough to become the village elder he would change this part of the story to make it more believable.

"Yes," the village elder said, "the men of this strange army wore skirts. For they were a mighty warrior tribe who didn't care what anyone thought of them. The Snatcher sent forth her Army of Blue Men to smite both armies. But the armies, seeing they were allies with a common enemy, joined forces and rampaged through the streets of That Lunn Don. They destroyed what they could destroy, chanting 'Can't pay won't pay,' as they battled their way toward The Snatcher's fortress with pitchforks and flaming torches.

"Many lives were lost in the ensuing bloody battle, and the armies were ultimately defeated, but the message had been sent. No longer would Yarksher put up with the tyranny of The Snatcher. The Snatcher was forced to recant her new tax, and abdicated her throne in shame soon after.

She went to live in exile, where she was never heard from again for another generation.

"Scar Gill spent many years in search of The Snatcher's hiding place, so he could avenge The Under-dwellers and the people of Yarksher for the wrongs done to them. But his search proved futile and The Snatcher remained in hiding.

"Until one day, long after Scar Gill had given up his quest, one of The Snatcher's cohorts announced she was dead and ordered the country to mourn for her passing. There was much rejoicing throughout the land of Yarksher, and street parties were held in celebration. The surviving Under-dwellers looked forward to the day when they could visit The Snatcher's grave and urinate on it, but The Snatcher's cohort decreed that she should be burned at the stake and her ashes sealed in a vault to protect them.

"Some say, before she died, The Snatcher passed her spirit to a new body, leaving an empty shell behind, so that she could continue her evil work from beyond the grave. Others say she made a pact with the devil and lives on to this day, plotting her revenge on the people of Yarksher, using the scabbed ones to do her bidding just as she did during her reign of terror. Nobody knows for sure.

"And so we remain vigilant, and watch out for the scabbed ones. We guard our homes, we guard our sheep, and we guard our children's milk. Because these things are important to us. And we will never let them be taken from us again."

"Amen," chanted a chorus of children.

"Amen," whispered Scar Gill to himself. He looked out to his sheep, satisfied himself they were safely grazing in their field.

A flutter of movement in a nearby bush caught Scar Gill's attention. He watched, raising himself up from the ground. A stranger, his hairless, naked body covered in scabs and boils, darted out from the bush.

"Scabbed ones!" Scar Gill shouted. He pulled an axe from his belt and ran at the stranger.

Printed in Great Britain
by Amazon

Rapids, MI: Baker Book House, 1964), 6. Spurgeon is here commenting on a section of Mark's Gospel.
15. A lot of these examples are given in fairly black and white terms. I readily acknowledge that there are a host of "What ifs . . .?" that might be offered e.g. "What if the neighbour were swapping his tyres because he needed safely to drive his epileptic son to the hospital first thing on Monday morning and that son had a *grand mal* on Saturday night that prevented him from doing it then, and . . ." It is not my intention to play those kind of games, but to give broad, illustrative examples. Besides, hard cases make bad law, and – as we said – the purpose of this exercise is not to provide an exhaustive list of legitimate and illegitimate activities.
16. Not his official title!
17. Sutcliff, "The Authority and Sanctification of the Lord's-Day," 10, emphasis original.

CONCLUSION

1. Jonathan Edwards, *The Works of Jonathan Edwards* (Edinburgh: Banner of Truth, 1974), 2:94.